Under a Collapsing Sky

B. W. Teigland

AOS Publishing 2021

ISBN: 978-1-7775139-4-8

Cover Design: Rue Mader

Visit AOS Publishing's website:
www.aospublishing.com

"Brandon Teigland's *Under a Collapsing Sky* revels in the terrifying entanglement of life as it flies in the face of individualism as a survival strategy. His vision of a possible future is *so* possible that it fascinates as it horrifies, invading the mind and becoming the inescapable present. With uncommon insight and in searingly precise language, Teigland asks: if individuality is a mass delusion, and one that has led our species toward ruin, who, or what, will replace the 'I'? *Under a Collapsing Sky* is as much about our end as it is about the all too natural consequences of today's actions, an uncanny and prescient novel that responds to ongoing ecological and social crises in ways shockingly new while entirely of our moment."

—Kyle Flemmer, The Blasted Tree

I

It is beautiful to feel your heart throbbing.

But often the shadow feels more real than the body.

The samurai looks insignificant

beside his armour of black dragon scales.

—Tomas Tranströmer

2041, May

"It's like a biochemical form of emulation," Céline Høltermand said aloud into a digital voice recorder as she examined the specimen. Her brow formed an arrow between her eyes, pointing down to where her attention was focused. "The act of perfecting or surpassing that which is imitated. It's nothing until it encounters something. It survives by being taken in by the thing it wishes to become, to go beyond survival instinct, beyond endurance." *And lives as that thing,* she thought. *As a sort of brain parasite.*

This sample was the only sample she could obtain. She knew it was synthetic. It was created in a lab like her own, which made it hard to assess its original form. Plus, it wasn't anywhere near the pure form she needed but another variant, a vitiated version posing as the real thing. An inoculation centre, affiliated with this secret laboratory, was out there. The concentrate was out there. But she neither had the concentrate nor knew where to find it.

The government wouldn't even allow her work to be published. The censor quashed Céline and her University of California colleagues. The current parties were promising to legalize the drug before the end of their term, and her team's work directly opposed that promise. Which was upsetting, as their research could be forestalled or foreclosed for decades or perhaps, she feared, forever.

She was struck by her colleagues' lack of concern. It was possibly the end of their academic careers. Even so, they'd seemed completely unworried. As if none of it had anything to do with them. Although nobody was safer, not even they were untouchable. Obviously, it would take a few more weeks for this to sink in fully.

The drug, having been under assessment by the courts, was defaulted as an illegal substance by the United States of Europe and North America (USENA). Its growing popularity as a simple palliative, however, especially among those with terminal forms of illness, was rapidly changing people's minds.

Given that it was an illegal substance, research on it was limited to pharmacologically refined replicas: synthetics. The myths of its cure-all qualities in the unrefined forms could, therefore, not be challenged by the scientific community. Claims endorsing it as a cure for cancer, or at least some forms of cancer, were strengthened by the day. What frustrated Céline Høltermand more was that those who said these things, those making the most profit off their lies, were increasingly considered as representatives of the medical community itself. With equal measures of disappointment and disdain, she mechanically prepared a fresh glycerol stock to store the sample and then returned it to the lab fridge and verified that the temperature was still set at negative twenty degrees Celsius.

●

As Céline Høltermand and her colleagues' research inside the lab became more and more tied up in litigations, she found that her research outside of the lab was becoming investigative: she needed to find the natural substance. The university's board of directors—

who feared another strike could happen any day because of embargo decisions—asked Céline to take a vacation, and she decided that this would be an opportunity to delve deeper.

No one knew how the substance had entered the economy. Allegedly, it was first sold by a group out of British Columbia called Tears of the Phoenix, whose religion was the drug itself. When the cult was asked to prove their beliefs in the Supreme Court of Canada, they cited particular Old Testament passages that were faithfully interpreted as referring to the substance—that which anointed the One—which was the oil they made.

It didn't take long for their competitors, claiming to sell the original Phoenix Tears, to take the religion right out of it. Without religion, the drug created a sense of impending apocalypse, of a privatized apocalypse.

Céline Høltermand and her colleagues had decided to call their one and only sample 'Enoch', after the only human in the Old Testament to achieve emulation. They joked that God should take it from them as God took Enoch, so they wouldn't have to deal with the science.

Someone in a hoodie suggested they go for a much-needed synth-beer near campus. The vote was in: they were officially on strike. Céline Høltermand had never understood why scientists liked to drink so much, but she never refused an offer to bolster that sense of solidarity, even if it was in vain. Knowing herself as an isolated, solitary being, she had lost the desire to unite. Liquor was, perhaps, the perfect distraction. Without the assistance of alcohol, it was hard to understand other people, to know what secrets were hidden in their human hearts. Now that the USENA's heavy food-safety regulation had been placed on agricultural production, synthetic alcohol was all that was available. No one got very drunk with synthetic alcohol, anyway. *If it was play,* she thought, more in regards to her own ambiguous personality than to those around her, *it was serious play: serious and scientific.*

Now assailed by the empowering desire to live braver and truer than before the strike, her colleagues commenced with releasing the objects they had been thinking about for five long years of experimentation. Some large white rabbits leapt eagerly into the campus gardens, while others, in their peculiar stillness and watchfulness, lived in the scientists' houses as pets.

Céline Høltermand was the last one to leave. She returned to the lab, hung up her lab coat, with the "NO FUN" pin over the breast pocket, changed into her street clothes—which consisted of a heavily washed vintage band T-shirt and black denim overalls—and said goodbye to Enoch. She decided to start her vacation, aka investigation, tomorrow. She knew that she probably wouldn't be seeing the stranger for some time.

•

On her usual route home, Céline stopped at a food truck. Tooth fillings flashed in the proprietor's mouth. He was a Mexican man who ordered his kitchen staff around in Korean. He gripped a parabola-shaped Korean taco in his plump palm and placed it in

Céline Høltermand's thin hands. As she turned and walked away, she realized it would be a grave mistake to eat the taco: unable to find any indication that a USENA food-safety check had officially approved it, she knew it was probably not made with 100 percent lab-grown ingredients. She threw it out, along with her hunger, into the black plastic stomach of a trash bag.

She didn't eat anymore. Synthetic food usually contained a high amount of protein which was basically incompatible with her body's constitution. The surplus of indigestible amino acids from a cellular steak and a glass of wine, gene edited and fermented, was enough to make her feel like vomiting. She clutched her empty belly. The thought of food gave her shooting pains. Hunger circled her head like a vulture. The whole world, and everyone in it, were waiting to eat. First, they had waited for weeks. Now, they've been waiting for months. Hope was being eaten alive by hunger. *The world is hungry,* she thought, *and always will be.*

A fine cold rain was falling on the city. The weather had grown brisk, and she suddenly realized that, given the overall political situation in America, she was consumed with worry. In the street, she jammed her hands into her coat pockets. Her arms and legs were heavy. Her head, even heavier. She wasn't in good health. People were out on the streets, lined up in front of stores. The streets didn't look any different. People carried on as if nothing was wrong. You could tell that they no longer watched the news. *Why bother? Every day, things were getting worse.* She avoided the news, too. She needed to keep her reason from breaking down completely. She couldn't think of everything. She only had one head. Nonetheless, the news had spread to her about the secret breach in biosecurity between the West and the East. The affair was on the front pages of the newspapers—not only in the US, but also in Europe, and soon the rest of the world. On every channel across the planet, the bioplague was all they were talking about.

For some time now, she hadn't slept or dreamed. And the others? They went along without seeming to show any sign of impatience, without happiness, without sadness, without curiosity, without meaning. She didn't really know how other people felt anymore. But she began, all the same, to get seriously tired of being alone in the crowd.

Her apartment block was in old Koreatown. She wandered through the neighbourhood for an hour or more, but couldn't find any visible signs that indicated a change in the political regime. A Korean crowd thronged in front of one of those restaurants that occupied several floors or a whole building. There was the noise of orders yelled out. No one merely spoke. They all shouted the language. The smell of soup, roasted meat, herbs, jasmine, and charcoal fires came wafting out from the balconies and terraces of these buildings, where people looked down from the casino, gambling devices in hand. Others hurried along carrying baskets or pushing shopping carts full of kimchi, sticky rice, soybean or chili paste, still sold in the street rather than in any of the major food labs like SynBio.

Céline Høltermand slowly walked through a narrow alleyway until she reached a crimson painted door. The apartment house she rented was on the second floor of a pawnshop. The number twenty-three and one-half was there to greet her, as were the two vertical lines of black Korean characters painted on the door. She found the weekly food parcel delivery on her doorstep. In clear, authoritative typeface, the box's label read: "SynBio: Our pure compounds open billions of opportunities!" She inspected her key, its steel bit gleaming, and then, having made sure it was the right one, turned it twice to the right in the lock. *Click-click.* Her keys clinked metallically against one another as she swung the door open.

Her apartment was blank and empty. It was stark with its layers of white paint. There was just one of everything: one bed in the only bedroom; one small window in the kitchen with nothing but a bare table and a single chair; the sitting room with one TV, one armchair. The heater was broken, and the room was drafty. She felt cold so she left her coat on and tried not to notice. But she couldn't repress the shiver that was steadily growing inside.

Céline Høltermand found a brightly coloured scrap in the nearly empty pantry—a bit of SynBio wrapper from a food parcel with a four-by-three grid of uneaten squares. She snapped off an entire section and bit into the soft, dark mass. Then, she poured herself a glass of ink-white milk. The chemically synthesized milk substance took on either a white or a bluish tinge, depending on the faded yellow of the kitchen's lightly mixed shadows. The mixture was an emulsion of fatty acids, proteins, minerals, and sugars in water.

She looked out of the kitchen window onto the red neon signboard of the pawnshop. It proclaimed, "Red Dragon Art and Antiques," and lit the scaly bark and dusty leaves of a stunted palm tree. Photographs covered her apartment walls, or rather, copies of the same picture in various sizes. Each showed the same thing: a large skeleton structure made of aluminum tubes. She moved away from the window to inspect the photographs of the strange, airy dome with arches made of simple steel tubes bent to define a large hemisphere in space. She stared at the large glass panes that covered the hemisphere, studying the fixing of the joints, pressing her head closer to the pictures, straining her eyes, concentrating ever more intensely on them, until, it seemed, she had solved something. *A space surrounded by glass walls, a remarkably delicate contraption, a bubble of air, a dwelling,* she thought, as she moved from one image to the next. The architecture had etched itself, line by line, into her head and into her heart.

Several years back, Céline Høltermand had had no experience handling a camera, but she learned by shooting everyday things and watching tutorials. She had bought a 450-megapixel camera from a blissed-out twenty-something surfer dude, only to realize that it would be a thousand times better to just trade it in at the pawnshop downstairs for a much simpler DSLR model.

Loneliness and isolation fascinated her. In a world where everything and everyone was connected, the feeling of being alone, being herself, being uniquely herself, was her dilemma as a photographer. She was living on the other side of something. Only in photography, when the negative was developed, was something else revealed, something else caught by the snapshot: her presence was revealed. An image of what she was not, a powerful state of being negatively. For her, photography was the picture of a hollow, of a lack, of an absence.

Switching on the coloured light bulb in her room made the whole scene a metallic violet.

She dragged out her hundreds of thousands of notes from all her drawers and closets—stacks of notes, large and heavy—and spread them across the living room floor streaked in violet lighting. These notes had the sole purpose of helping her understand the evidence of her own existence. These were the things she would leave behind as proof of her having been here, should she suddenly vanish. *Because dilemmas destroy*, she thought.

Grey thoughts, incomplete ideas, and pointless grief confused and jumbled her memories. She was alone in the world and a stranger to herself, with the burden of feeling, having to feel, and having to absurdly translate the most painful feelings, the most piercing emotions. Ever since she had turned one of her last two pairs of pants into cash (cash that she used to purchase a cheap hair trim from an old Korean barber and a tarot card reading from a Spanish witch), she was always thinking, always feeling in translation.

The neighbourhood witch, who lived above a thrift store called The Broom Closet, had tried to reframe the negative tarot cards that she'd drawn from the deck in her reading of Céline Høltermand's fate. "Fate is not final," the witch had said about the cards, which were the most traditionally negative cards in the deck. Making connections or interpretations of their disturbing imagery was often discouraging.

Céline Høltermand had asked the witch if she could redraw, and despite the witch's reluctance to do so, she redrew anyway. "At least," Céline Høltermand had said, "until I find something I like." But they kept coming up negative.

First, it had been Death: the witch had said it traditionally meant loss, grief, or the ending of a cycle but could also mean crossing a threshold, a fresh start, a transformation, or rebirth. Then, the Tower: disaster, upheaval, destruction, breakdown—but reframed, destroying illusions, breakthrough, challenging outdated beliefs. Finally, the Ten of Swords: betrayal, backstabbing, a final ending—but reframed, no more suffering, the worst is over, the hidden is revealed, you can act without hiding. Céline Høltermand had pushed for just one more draw. Predictably, the draw produced yet another ominous card.

Seeing how the cards had been dealt and knowing that Céline Høltermand was probably as confused and panicked by her lot as anyone else would have been, the witch shuffled the deck of seventy-eight cards. She then delicately placed their fortunes back inside the velvety mouth of a blessed pouch and reassuringly said, "It is not what happens to us that determines how we live our lives, but the stories that we choose to tell ourselves." She caught Céline

Høltermand's eye and continued: "There is no way to erase negativity from our lives. Because if we did, it would destroy the balance and rid life of all meaning." The witch concluded by saying, "It would be better to turn bitterness into beauty."

Céline Høltermand couldn't remember what questions she had asked the witch then, nor could she fully recall what the answers had been. Some of her impressions of what happened after the witch spoke were so vague. It was only when she remembered those words afterwards, that she was aware of them at all. And even then, they were only a feeling of something, like beauty in a nightmare. Had she asked, *What am I? What shall I do? What can I believe and hope for?* No, she couldn't be sure that she had divided herself up in such a sphinxlike way. The whole experience, like a dream now closed, had gently bound its white blindfold of false memories about her eyes.

She went to the kitchen. The apartment creaked beneath her feet. She placed herself in front of the molecular coffee machine, leaning against a cabinet door while she waited for the light to flash on. Then she shoved a mug into place, and precisely 8-ounces of a slightly overheated brown liquid spurted out. It was a liquid almost entirely unlike coffee. She cradled the warmth of the mug in her hands, downing about a third of the drink in a single swallow. Beanless basic molecules. Coffee made from the chemical components of various food particles. She thought she could taste the sunflower husks, or maybe it was watermelon seeds, beneath the artificial flavouring.

She crossed the kitchen to the window and lit a herbal cigarette. It contained a mixture of flowers that she had grown herself—mostly rose and mugwort—at a vacant lot that people had started to use as an urban garden. Smoking these medicinal herbs, she might have believed that she felt better, having been able to breathe for a minute. It was three in the morning, but as always, the night at the window was watching her. The hundreds of high-rises, medium-sized buildings, and apartment complexes had all gone black. She pressed her forehead against the cool glass and closed her eyes.

Sitting down at the table under the kitchen's electric ceiling light, she smoked her herbal cigarette as hard as she could. Taking deeper and deeper drags. Wishing that the embargo would loosen up enough for her to have a real tobacco cigarette. When she had drunk enough molecular coffee and returned to the room, the apartment had changed. The light wasn't the same. It went from violet to green.

Céline Høltermand frowned for a fitful instant at the stack of notes, and then began reading them, note after individual note. Then she returned to her thoughts. There was an email she'd been expecting for the last few weeks. Six months ago, she had requested the coroner's reports from the offices of numerous state medical examiners. All of the reports were about people belonging to a loosely affiliated group of political extremists who had committed suicide immediately after voting in the sixty-fourth presidential election. A disruption in the electoral process was not without political implications: a suspended election, military guarded polls, etc. The reports had arrived with appended documents (which she had to go above her own research clearance to get authorized): the autopsy reports, the toxicology reports, the police reports, and the medical records.

She turned toward her computer screen and went over the email.

Autopsies were performed on the bodies... their brains and peripheral nervous systems were examined carefully and were found to contain a mysterious substance: produced inside nerve tissue in infinitesimal quantities, it appears to be a protective secretion that built up gradually... immaterial, brainstem-like entities, suggesting telepathy as a form of contagion...

Possessing samples of the parasitic fungus that were linked to the genetically contaminated food, Céline Høltermand and her colleagues had discovered this new chemical compound, which (from what the coroner's reports seemed to suggest), when introduced into the bloodstream, penetrated the brain and, without damaging the grey matter, kept the parasite alive while immunizing the organism against the human body. She considered her sample from the lab: an extremely resistant variety of bacteria able to withstand water loss, fluctuations in temperature, and brief periods outside the brain, in any environment. It was clear that the bacteria and the fungus were related to the new chemical substance, but the only thing that could link them was the introduction of a third agent: a plasmid. In short, whoever was responsible for the genetics behind the contamination had managed to create a unique species of microorganism that parasitized the brain by gradually changing the chemical effects of this extremophile.

It was a stranger, an incomprehensible stranger, a stranger full of secrets, a secret forced among all the other ghosts of science, an enemy, Céline Høltermand thought, as she moved from the piles of disorganized notes strewn over the living room floor to another part of that same room. Then she reached into each of the formerly sewn shut, fake pants pockets that she had recently unstitched herself and searched until she touched something flat and round and sticky.

She sent the solid metal disk with its ribbed rim bowling into the coin-operated telemeter TV in the corner of the living room and chose one of the three channels by turning the dial on the attachable box. She had discovered the antediluvian machine among shelves of useless junk at the pawnshop. Never watching what was playing on the TV, she used it to create a bit of white noise so that the loud, monotonous, uninterrupted creaking of the pawnshop's doors opening and closing wouldn't be quite so loud. The screen was alive with rapid, jerky, flickering images. The sound of the TV at night was a soothing, nocturnal sound. The programming—a loop of news, cartoons, and advertisements—faded and then brightened so that the room pulsed and twitched with neurotic light. She felt as if she were submerged in water and drowning in it.

Céline Høltermand had nothing but self-contact, and when there wasn't that, there was nothing. She went through life without joy and mystery, and because of this, time seemed brief. The void, easy. With blatant anti-eroticism towards her erotic value, she aimed for the neutral life that lives and moves, to be full of the neutral busy pleasure. The purely neutral Céline Høltermand went on dates with herself, was romantic with herself, bought herself gifts, took herself and her DSLR camera on vacations, like her vacation to Arizona, where she'd taken the picture of the biome, which now hung on the walls of her apartment.

But Céline Høltermand had failed to demystify that mute and incomprehensible triangle between her legs. She had gone through phases of being asexual, anti-sexual, and auto-sexual, then phases where she looked at her simple body with no expression whatsoever, no desire for pleasure from herself or others. Her triangular dream was impenetrable. *Sex is childish,* she thought, *but love does the most harm.*

Only the dead embryos of some unknown desire were cradled there, inside the three-pointedness of her maternal darkness. Ugly and vengeful.

She pulled out her camera from inside her canvas haversack covered in metal pinback buttons and, turning it on herself, took a picture of her face and, with a bit of guilty curiosity, snapped another of her sex. Her grey-green expression in the photograph was withdrawn. She had an average forehead, the eyebrows also average, the eyes, the nose, the mouth, the chin... the only unusual feature was the red macula covering it. Despite the stain, it was a completely closed-off face that failed to leave a memory. She only had to shut her eyes to forget it. And then open them again to be ignored because of it.

The finer features of Céline Høltermand's face had collapsed too early in her life. Between twenty and thirty, her face had not kept the same contours as it had had in its youth. It had suddenly grown older. She had once been that other woman. In a sense, she still was. *How long can a presentation last?* Her face appeared to be a frightful inversion of the life she was leaving behind. But instead of being dismayed by this, she realized that she preferred the image of her ruined face. Because it was the face she recognized most. And with it, she felt the power of a consuming interior force.

In the other case, the image of her sex was exposed, strangely real. It gave her the impression of being connected to something eternal, to the functioning of the whole, as though it were a tunnel opening onto the infinite essence of the world. She felt nostalgia for this companion simply because she had lived with it for so long. Whether they lived well or badly hardly mattered. It wasn't a grotesque fragment of her body, like the Orcus mouth of Sacro Bosco, neither was it an immobile and indifferent hole for despair to be carried around in an excess of suffering. Their past was beautiful because it was feminine. So would be their future. Only the present hurt.

The light redshifted, and so too did her mood. Taking out a pair of safety shears from the desk drawer and then unraveling a bundle of jute rope that was hanging on the wall above her bed, she began to tie herself up in shibari. Silently threading the evening's harness, she intentionally positioned each of the knots and ties along the pressure points on her body, all following ancient somatosensory patterns, with small, intuitive variations, entering a subspace of submission, control, and mystical ecstasy. And for a brief interval of time, her body belonged to her.

With her eyes now closed, she began to dissolve into a sound: the even meter of a vividly convincing documentarian's voice on the TV that kept talking and talking. This voice, photographically speaking, created a picture in her mind's eye and seemed to be telling a story, a history: the mythology of a country, the Great Kingdom of Singapura, its tiger-towns in the forbidden hills, and the were-tigers that inhabited them. The words, sentences, voice, and speech morphed into an entirely different order, a meaningless order—before sleep swallowed her up.

•

By nine thirty in the morning she was ready to go. She took no time in packing, assembling enough clothing to last her a week or so. She also packed her laptop, the camera, tinctures of concentrated herbal extract, and a stash of SynBio bars.

Riding the Pacific Coast Highway cliffs on a mild, windless day, driving toward what would be either another imitator or the genuine cult of the Tears of the Phoenix, Céline Høltermand listened. Listened, for the thousandth time, to the posted conference talk she had given on the history of consciousness. The talk had been horribly rated. Scorned all over the country. Said to be "virtually meaning-free," "contradicting itself hundreds of times," and "vaporous and infuriating." People wanted only bad science, misinformation, and she had none of that to give them.

"We are all of us full of alien life-forms with which we ourselves can communicate in only a very limited way. Often, we destroy these things because they refuse to share what they are with us, and in the end, pose only a threat to humankind. Other times, we find ways of coexisting with them, by limiting miscommunication and reaping what benefit we may."

She clenched her teeth; her molars fused together with the stress. A kind of looming anticipation hung in the air like a dark hope. Outside the city, lines of SynBio trucks stretched for miles and miles. For a few minutes she attempted to contemplate the natural beauty of the steamy landscape, but as the road wound around cheerful sunlit meadows and woods, then rolling fields and forests, she soon lost interest and turned her attention back to the talk.

"We are invaded and in turn invade. A cell is infinitely different from us and yet it still is essentially us—it shares the same essence but not the same form. When it becomes dysfunctional, and as a consequence we become sick, this feature becomes obvious." The room dark. The audience watching. The talk recorded. The mortification of listening to it again, palpable. She could hear the slide in the recording change from one of her brilliant photographs to another.

Her photos had an unusual air, especially those taken outside the lab: the gigantic latticework of a tower looming in the morning fog, or the wooden carcass of a Viking ship abandoned in a former ocean basin turned prairie, or the ecological monsters that were sometimes revealed when dividing an object into mirror images of itself, or a drag queen posing outside a metallic building.

"But what if there was an organism that was able to trick the mind into believing it was something it's not? An organism that mirrored information and reflected only what you wanted it to be?

"Such an organism would show you one thing and hide the other. If you were terminally ill, and you wanted to be cured, it would pretend to cure you. And whoever you made contact with would see what you see.

"But what about after death? Doesn't this mean that you will still seem alive after the illness has compromised the biological system? We speculate that one in four people who uses the drug known as Phoenix Tears is already dead, and yet we see them living. How is this possible? The short answer is, it's not." She could hear the sound of people getting up to leave, of people walking out.

"Stranger yet, others have claimed to have been reincarnated into something other than human. Changed into another form entirely, while retaining the same essence, for the duration of the experience. This too is impossible." The wind coming in from the driver-side window cynically flicked her fringed bangs and lifted the lapels of her leather coat.

"What do we think? What is our explanation? We think the organism works on the level of collective hallucinations. That the delusions are individual in nature but can create free associations with others within an ever-expanding social group of those using Phoenix Tears.

"Its effects weaken over time, but this is not because of any tolerance. Its immunity becomes part of the user's immunity. It stays in your system, produces itself as though it were a natural biochemical agent in the brain. An alternate version of the brain within the brain, another brain, if you will, resting on top of the original. An alternate body within the body; in other words, another reality wired and routed into the nervous system. Eventually, every cell is replaced, and you are a new organism.

"We don't know how intelligent it is. It seems to lack creativity. It could be that all it does is mimic the information it has access to. We don't know, but with our research, we wish to find out. Thank you."

In the moment, she cringed and shrank at the level of applause. No wonder she'd been blacklisted. Her audience had followed the civil war between altered-right and altered-left news channels. It was the William Buckley and Gore Vidal news debates of the sixties all over again. Though, it wasn't crypto-fascist anymore, not hidden admiration or support, but naked fascism. Agitation, lies, dirt.

The trip was beginning badly: all the rest stops had been closed along her route, and yet another inconvenience awaited her at the border. The white letters on the gigantic, reflective, rectangular, plastic-and-aluminum sheets, held up by round steel columns standing on either side of the national border crossing, had been vandalized: "You are now leaving Amerika," and on the other side, "You are now entering Kanada," both blacked over with spray-painted *k*'s. *People picked sides*, she thought. *It was too easy not to. But, in a sense, there are no sides.* She considered this as she dealt with the border guards who mechanically commented with bland, vacuous expressions and slowly motioned her over the national line. *There are no sides. To pick the better candidate now is to simply deal with a worse candidate later. The conservatives don't conserve anything, the liberals aren't liberating anyone, and everywhere the centre was lost.*

Her audience knew she had no evidence to back up her research, and even if they didn't know, they were more than likely to act the same way because of their allegiances. She had analyzed the insane properties of the drug, but she had no idea what it was composed of or what long-term effects it had on its users. She needed to find the Tears of the Phoenix. If anyone could give her answers about the experience, it was them. She hoped the rumours weren't true; she hoped they were still human.

●

The sun rose again, and she reached her destination. However, it was becoming colder and colder since she had crossed the border into Canada. It was the end of spring but the weather was overcast, the acreage appeared abandoned and the house's exterior rather sinister. In the distance, the large and wrinkled masses of rocks and mountains like white-crested waves rose, and closer a redwood forest circled in a Fibonacci sequence around the property.

It's odd to see redwoods in British Columbia, Céline Høltermand thought. *They haven't been here for thousands of years, yet with the profound changes in climate, maybe... They must have been planted by whoever lives here. But how did they grow so quickly?*

Old, junked vehicles were parked on the front lawn near a house, and set back from the house was what appeared to be a chapel. The hand-carved door of this chapel—*probably made of felled redwood,* she thought—caught her attention. On that door was a phoenix and, juxtaposing it, a life-size opalescent statue of the crucifixion spread its smooth white marble arms over her.

Céline Høltermand could smell the aerosol salts coming off the ocean as she shut the door of her vehicle. She took with her only a camera, which she wore loosely around her neck. It had been a long drive up, but it looked like this could be the spot, guarded and protected by solitude.

No one answered her knock, and she stood expectantly at the door of the strange house—strange because it seemed to be built of the tiny white roots mushrooms have. She started to wonder what she was doing there, feeling that she carried around with her the vulnerability of a solitary traveler. Then, she left the front step and began to walk the property, stepping over monster roots and huge knots, gnarled knots that looked like the faces of Greek gods and the paws of lions spread out at the redwood trees' bases.

Buffeted by the blue wind, a butterfly fluttered and beat crumpled wings. She began to notice the abundance and variety of fungi, a honeybee growling in the forests of corpse-grey and cloud-blue moss, and what could have been a variety of slime mould: a strange, alien-like structure in colour and form.

She took pictures of the oddly textured life-forms and thought about what it would be like to think the way they looked. It was a strange thought. They were almost like flowers in that they showed their entire consciousness, but they were not really the same. No, not the same at all. These fruiting bodies, unlike flowers, had a forbidden quality to them. And behind that quality, perhaps a forbidden knowledge.

When she checked the photos on the camera's screen, they looked damaged. Flickering black, white, or red. *Ghost pictures.* Céline Høltermand frowned but attributed it to some faulty mechanism in the camera itself. It had never done this before. She tried again and got more of the same results.

She became aware of webs in the hollow redwood stumps. The logs were woven into cocoons, but the spider itself was absent. Céline Høltermand knew of a species of spider, *Pimoa cthulhu,* that lived in the California redwood forest lands, a habitat similar to this one. She imagined the work of the spider, which was probably flattened in its secret corners that allowed it to remain properly advised of every slight tremor, each microscopic shift in the all-but-invisible network.

This place was not part of the Anthropocene, Céline Høltermand thought, as she moved with great care so that the creaking of her leather jacket wouldn't drown out any noise that might come from the deeper brush. *The Anthropocene has already ended here, but not anywhere else—in this spot alone, it has ended. But if the Anthropocene has ended, then this must be the start of something else. Something where human and nonhuman refugees from environmental disasters come together. Like these trees, these fungi, and these spiders.* Her face steeled at the next thought: *Or else it was the Cthulhucene, the time where humanity shall be devoured by an enormous horror of its own making. Caught in a web of vacancies.*

She still didn't see the spider and hoped she wouldn't—because she knew that that event could go either way. Like the groundhog and its shadow was a harbinger of spring, the empty webs of the spider seemed to be an early sign of whatever came next.

The incline was becoming steeper and steeper. Her ears pricked at the soft crumble of pine needles and branches popping underfoot, and she caracoled toward it. Scanning the empty space, she finally spotted a figure struggling toward her, making his way around the base of the giant trees on the hillside. He was clambering up the slope, occasionally collapsing on his hands and dragging his left leg after him. She swooped in from above and grabbed the man by the shoulder, linking her body to his in an attempt to keep him from falling.

Once he regained his good foot, she could see that his face was eclipsed by the broad brim of a hat. Under it, a red beard bubbled frightfully out of his collar. When he removed his hat in a gesture of thanks, his hair wisped out in wiry strands from its ponytail, moving like moss raining down from an angel oak tree. The fragile human was so many times thinner than everything else in this wood; the hugeness of the deceivingly ancient trunks and their cities of branches, in what could have been sky, shrunk him into a secret sight that only she could see.

He carried a wicker basket on his back and a walking stick in his hand. Like a wizard's staff, the stick was long and smooth, capped with the wings of a phoenix, carved from wood reminiscent of the redwood on the chapel door. Although the man didn't show it, Céline Høltermand was inclined to believe he had seen her first.

"I no longer sell Phoenix Tears, if that's what you're after. I'm sure you can find some other place," the bearded man said in a reedy voice. He didn't stop walking. He seemed determined to get back to his mysterious business, the walking stick jabbing the ground as he went.

Céline Høltermand, sensing the unwelcoming tone in the man's voice, stated her purpose with as much candor as she could summon: "I don't want any. I just need to know what it's made of and, if you are the original supplier, where you got the first batch. Out of what lab and under what authority was it originally made?"

At this, the bearded man stopped. She could see the wisdom in his deep, dark eyes flicker and sensed a very different nature that lay hidden inside him. In his curt, imperious voice, he said, "What interest is it of yours? Are you a scientist?"

"Psychochemist," she answered quickly, and then noticed him looking at the camera now dangling from her left shoulder "and amateur photographer. I mostly take photos of my and my colleagues' work." She realized she was nervous, veering, and demurely returned to the point. She didn't want to let herself feel discomfort, a sensation that always came to her whenever she talked about herself. She often awkwardly cited herself as if her name had been put in quotation marks. Abruptly, with physical displeasure, she started thinking about how the man must have seen the defect: the red birthmark covering her otherwise clean, average face.

"I'm not after your recipe," she continued, uncertainly, and waited for a moment. "Actually, I only want to know its origin—and maybe what came just before its origin. Where it started and what it's doing here."

Pause.

He didn't answer. He stopped, looked at her, waiting for an explanation. When she gave none, and no one answered, the interval of silence became embarrassing. She saw the crazed, obsessed look in his frighteningly intelligent eyes. Red eyes that were burning, shining, like a wild animal the moment before an attack. And all of a sudden, she realized that he was still deeply involved in whatever amateur terrorist movement had caused all of this societal disruption and political strife. Perhaps, he might even be one of its leaders. For all she knew, he not only knew about the secret lab leakages but was the one who decided to keep them a secret.

The old man dressed in furs stood near her, with his craggy face like that of a trapper's, and he began digging patiently around a corpulent organism in the soil. Then, armed only with his modest knife, he began to saw through the stem, a meter in diameter, run through with stalk-like fibres. The look on old man's face was at once wise and cruel. She knew that he had time on his side. He was moved by no precise motivation, but rather an animal-like obstinacy. She attributed to him the intuitive knowledge and powers of a shaman.

The foundations of the world were going to collapse. The empty future of space was coming; it was approaching and sought to devour them. No other reason impelled him to trust her with his memories, except maybe the profound instinct to unearth what might have otherwise been forgotten. The man hoped to penetrate her soul for the truth in her words. And, like someone accustomed to silence, he spoke shortly: "I'll show you. But you'll have to spend the night and share the company of a stranger."

The night must have been following on his heels, for just as he said this, the colours of the woods deepened in shade.

•

His name was Johannes Van Vyferyken. He was tall and solidly built. With his long, grey, dirty hair, and his mismatched clothing in a state of disarray, he inspired a sort of pitying respect. He led her to the strange structure she had knocked at when she first arrived. Inside, the place was crammed and clogged with a fantastic conglomeration of things. From his wicker backpack he pulled out mushrooms, which he then prepared for a soup and cooked, with very little of anything else besides some fresh herbs, in a bubbling stewing pot placed directly over the heat of the hearth.

"Don't worry. This variety is nontoxic."

Céline Høltermand took a sip after he ladled the steaming liquid into her bowl. "It tastes like chicken," she said. Not wanting to point out the obvious, she slurped the rest of her words.

"Well, they don't call it chicken of the woods because it tastes like snail. You can find it almost anywhere in the world," Johannes Van Vyferyken said. His speech had a downy sound. And through the beard came a smile. It was not the smile of a young man; it had in it an elliptic, untamed wisdom that could afford to be gentle. It could be tolerant because it had seen so much.

The two sat in silence for a while. The glints made by the fire in the grate danced, picking out the capricious lines of Johannes Van Vyferyken's mouth and nostrils. His face took on the boney aspect of everything around him, and for a moment, Céline Høltermand thought his features were no different from the shapes of mycelium in the wall, like ghosts hovering behind him. He did not breathe, or at least he seemed not to. The fire flickered at the black shadows of objects frozen and motionless, and instantly she became as silent and still as he was. When the crackling of the wood turned into a hissing, he picked up the cast-iron tongs and banged them against the logs. Only then did he speak, and he kept on speaking for a long time.

"No-o"–Johannes Van Vyferyken sounded unsure–"this place is not the origin. Though the source of the mystery runs heavily through here." He smoked his pipe, also redwood. The oxbowing tobacco smoke gave off a pleasing smell, and Céline Høltermand breathed in deeply.

"It was a mistake for me to have taken it. To have brought it here." His anxious voice came from deep inside the larynx's two-inch tube-shaped organ between the pharynx and trachea. "But at the time, I was worried only about the safety of those whom I worked with on the project. And foolishly, I did what I did." Absorbed in listening, Céline Høltermand hardly reacted but for uncrossing her legs. The floor was strewn with various animal skins. It was like being in a hunting lodge. On the wall was a rack for his guns. The metal shone with a gentle glow, tinted orange by the fire.

"I came to the project hoping to use the organism as a biofabrication agent. Just like this house, which was manufactured by this mycelium agent, as was the furniture. But the same facility was used by multiple companies, and the pharmaceutical industry got in there and messed things up for all of us. They bought us and everyone else out, repurposed our labs, and showed us the door."

She glimpsed his fingers fidgeting with his unbuttoned coat as if they were playing the story with the neck of a cello.

"I was furious, and all legal routes available to me were exhausted. So I broke into the third expedition. They were doing all kinds of psychotropic experiments, like what you'd imagine the American government did with LSD in the fifties—mind control or psychochemical warfare, whatever it was they were up to then. Really, Biosphere II was a facility for researching space colonization. But in every experiment designed to simulate exposure to deep space-time, it was the psyches of the human subjects, the biospherians themselves, that were most prone to disintegration during space exploration. Everything else—the facility and the life-support system—was just engineering, just mathematics, numbers..."

The fingers of his right hand stopped fiddling with his coat. She could now see an angular profile with cutaneous lesions under the scraggly beard and a mouth that twitched from words as from a tic. His eyes, edgy and incalculable, made her think of the cracked green pupils of a fox.

"The serum was designed to control the Mars colonists over long periods of space travel. Space is the most unforgiving environment for the human psyche. Space is one big deprivation chamber withholding even the most minimum amount of sensory input, and the psyche needs to remain functional. Most importantly, space has been cultureless until now. An entire renaissance could take place between Earth and the next habitable planet, outside the dead seven of our solar system. But how do you control an entire culture? How do you prevent the interstellar equivalent of the

Russian Revolution from occurring? You put all minds into one mind. So that 'apart from' becomes 'a part of.'"

Then Johannes Van Vyferyken, whose chin had been propped on the handle of his walking stick while he had been seated, began to rise, becoming a vertically oriented biped, and looked out of the black windows. "Come with me. I'll show you the rest."

•

The cave where he took her was slightly off from the heavily forested spot they had first met. The blue circle of his lantern's eye glided down through tangled threads of night, and the iridescent fungi along the path to the cave provided the necessary additional light to guide them through the dark hour. In the thermotolerant cave, more of the same phosphorescent shapes grew. For Céline Høltermand, it was like walking through a kaleidoscope, so full and bright with patterned life-forms.

"As you might appreciate, the eukaryotic organisms here thrive because they are from a moon that no longer supported life." Johannes Van Vyferyken's voice echoed beyond that empty and dark cave room, and farther still, into many more empty and dark caverns and galleries. "On their moon, the atmosphere, climate, and gravity changed considerably: too cold in the night, too warm in the day, always too dry, and in the last extremity, they sporified repeating the desperate cycle as best they could until their spores found their way to Earth. I'm still not sure how that happened. It was a long time ago, before there was life on Earth. They might have triggered it. I don't know.

"But here," he continued, his eyes corrupted and dim in the glow, "they carry on the continuity of their species. A kind of mobile fungus with a fully ripe intelligence. They just need a warm and dense atmosphere. Soil, moisture, and time. Actually, the life cycle of this fungus still depends a lot on the phases of the moon, though not as much as on their alien ecology."

His lantern pointed at the ground like an enormous blue-lacquered fingernail. Then the ground quivered, here and there, and out came undulating yellow lumps, a multitude of spheres gummed into a mass, automatically.

"Those ones are going through their final phase. Even for them, there is no actual distinction—they all are, and none of them is the same organism. You can see why Space Biosphere Ventures took an interest in them. They are, by trade, decomposers and amplify the otherwise gradual development of whatever biome they occupy through the secretions and fertilizers they release."

"Is that why this redwood forest seems more ancient than it is?" Céline Høltermand asked.

"Y-yes"—again, Johannes Van Vyferyken sounded unsure—"I planted the redwoods when I arrived. They're perfect for this climate, and the tannins that give the bark its reddish hue protect against fire and insects and, of course, the fungi."

Céline Høltermand felt the vitality of the area as they walked back toward the house. She looked up through the canopy of trees. Its fractal pattern against the constellations stirred primordial emotions she wished she knew more about.

"And the drug?" she asked, unsatisfied.

"The eukaryote was the obvious choice for terraforming, as it not only accelerates the diverse growth of a biome—well under two years within a closed system—but can also biofabricate structures that are sustainable and fully integrated into the ecosystem. Other divisions in Biosphere II took a separate approach. They broke down the organism and synthesized its intelligence, altered the organic chemistry. Used it for its telepathic abilities."

"Wha-at"—this was it, she was asking the one question she hadn't been able to answer for herself because of the censor on her research—"about the brain bacteria?"

He made no reply, as if there was a riddle under his crown, next to the question. A riddle made up of the question's answer, an answer older, more desolate, destitute, and dismal than all the expanding and multiplying questions. And then he replied: "By investigating the highly complex and elusive fauna of the brain, by imitating patient gardeners, the bacteriologists of the pharmaceutical division obtained various species and subspecies of brain bacteria. Even though in a scientific sense this species X remained a thermophilic eukaryote, and so could be categorized into any of the few truly thermotolerant bacteria, archaea, or fungi, we still didn't know how it lived optimally as an inhabitant of the brain. So these bacteria were collected in the form of ordinary gelatinous cultures inside sealed glass bacteria-breeders. And then they were administered on, well, a test specimen, a 3D-printed homunculus: organs without a body.

"The asexuality of the microorganisms had the advantage of hybridizing bacteria that settled on the thinnest parts of the brain, that clustered where nerves emerged from under the cerebral cortex, or along the nodes of Ranvier, producing in twenty-four hours—"

He interrupted himself with a long series of coughs, as if a never-felt-before anxiety had caught in his dry throat. Then he continued in a somewhat fainter voice, "Producing in twenty-four hours as many generations of bacteria as in experiments with domestic animals requiring millenniums, or even humanity since *Homo* Sapiens. These infinitesimal predators fed on the energy-producing discharge of nerve cells. They intercepted the brain's signals, using them to fuel their own minuscule bodies. In other words, blocking up all the brain's windows to the world."

When they got back to the yard of the biofabricated house of mycelium, Johannes Van Vyferyken turned toward the chapel and pushed open the door that had the phoenix carved deeply into it. Inside, veiled over with a light tissue of web, were several rows of pews and a pulpit, which could serve a small congregation. Under the pulpit was a door.

They took the stairs revealed by the open door, descending into a laboratory hidden beneath the chapel. For a second, Céline

Høltermand had forgotten the man had been a very successful scientist, but this subterranean lab reminded her of it. There were shelved samples of specimens with obscure labels, mostly fungi but also moss and lichen and other plants; nurseries containing swarms of bacteria, thousands of species, glowingly alive in transparent plexiglass shelving.

He disappeared into a room that leaked a cold mercury light at the end of the shelves and came back with a bag.

"The real Phoenix Tears," he said, tossing the bag at her. She caught it clumsily. "The recipe is on the package."

Once above again, sitting in the pews of the chapel, cold incense in the air, Céline Høltermand asked, "What happened to your followers?"

Johannes Van Vyferyken considered this for a moment, his beard accenting his Old-Testament look, and then spoke. "Playing away the truth. Taking whatever shape they like, whether it be human or animal, cloud or tree. Playing at a thousand beings.

"That's why I chose the phoenix as our emblem—the sacramental oil is like a spell of changing, of reincarnation. And if you delight in taking the shape of a bear, so that the bear grows in you and the human dies away and you become the bear, then the price is only the peril of losing one's self. Most stayed too long in their form, and the longer a human stays, the greater the peril."

"How many?" Céline Høltermand asked, all the while wanting to ask why they had made the change and he had not.

"Let me put it to you this way: many wise humans have forgotten their wisdom in becoming whales. Others wear the raven's wings and look through the raven's eyes and, forgetting their own thoughts, know only what the raven knows. But that is the way of this religion. I try to teach responsible usage of the sacrament, but some decide in the end that they were never meant to be human and become what they become."

The chapel seemed too human for the religion it was built to serve. Céline Høltermand wondered about the substance, comparing how it was being used in the cities, as a medicalized drug, with how it was being used here, as a consecrated element or Host or Eucharist.

As if reading her mind, Johannes Van Vyferyken spoke her thoughts: "The sacrament is our God because it allows the worshipper a choice in deciding where it wants the soul to go next. It is a generator of dreams, and brings life out of life. Space Biosphere Ventures wanted to use it only as a means to an end, as a utilitarian solution to space travel. And worse still, people in the cities, who have created so many derivatives of my recipe, have made it hard to determine with certainty what will happen to them in the end."

As she was leaving the next morning, Céline Høltermand noticed the animals—deer, birds, rabbits. And there were probably others that she did not notice. She said no words to them, knowing they had no human speech in them now.

Some of the creatures were roaming at the back of the chapel in the cemetery, which consisted of only a few nameless gravestones. Fungus grew on the plots, and inscribed on the few tombstones was the same epitaph: "All are born but not all are reborn as themselves."

She left, not knowing whose bodies were buried there. Or if there were any bodies at all.

2040, September

"I need your ID," said the transgender membership assistant at the dispensary counter. "Do you have a membership? Medical documents?" The assistant had trinkets woven into their white dreadlocks, metal and wooden hardware in their face, and, without looking at the deformed hands of the next "patient," nonetheless acknowledged his hands as "the problem."

"No." Gordon Nerdrum stared at the bold black lettering of the nonsense syllable on the assistant's name tag: Zez. Not because he couldn't decide whether this person was a he or a she—doing so would have never occurred to him—but because what he thought he was doing was illegal, and so he stared nervously ahead of him. Polite through ignorance.

"Can I have the information forms we had you fill out while you were waiting?"

The assistant took the double-sided laminate sheet that Gordon Nerdrum offered over the counter. Its many former uses ghosted through like a whiteboard at a school. His markered lines of print were smudged and shakily written. Some of the blue ink had rubbed off on the man's beige pleated pants. The assistant began inputting the information into the computer.

"Do you need a diagnosis? We can pull up our on-hand medical professional here on the screen." It was a stupid question; of course he had a diagnosis, but the membership assistant was required to offer the complimentary service to every customer.

Deferring to expert authority, as people often did, made things easier.

Gordon Nerdrum indicated his consent with a slight nod. His brittle spine was not about to do much more than that.

In a moment the medical professional was on the large, bright screen. The assistant twisted the monitor with the floating head toward the patient.

"Hello. What seems to be bothering you?"

"My... uhm... rheumatoid arthritis." Gordon Nerdrum held up his rootlike hands so that the webcam had the ability to see him.

"Doesn't look like they treated you the way they would have today. Old medicine was bad medicine. No one suffering from arthritis experiences deformity anymore."

"No. At the time, in my twenties, I was serving as physician on a military ship called the... Well, I've forgotten the name of the ship. Crap. Anyways, they gave me Aspirin. I've lived with this pain in my bones for over forty years. I'm tired. I can't sleep anymore. And after my wife passed, I said to hell with it."

Gordon Nerdrum was a rigid-faced man, stooped with round shoulders. His physical appearance inspired dislike. It was based on his peculiar, shambling walk. He had not the walk of a well man, but of a violently sick man. Sick in a sense that most had not experienced before.

"Well, I don't see why we can't help you. With the sleep and the pain, that is. Shouldn't be a problem to cure that. Mourning is another thing altogether. But like they say, our moral standard depends very much on our health. Yes, I think the treatment will do wonders for you, physiologically speaking."

The medical professional had already given the OK for the prescription, and a moment later, it flung out of the printer at the membership assistant.

The screen returned to the monitor's default background display: a high-resolution image of a translucent tear-shaped silvery drop with what appeared to be an elongated appendage; the appendage extended itself with a dim form of what might be referred to as rudimentary consciousness. It gave the impression that it was looking at its own microscopic shadow. Its oblong body lit up in deep blues, purples, and oranges, like the globular mixture of water, mineral oil, paraffin wax, and carbon tetrachloride in a lava lamp. The microcosm seemed sublime, yet Gordon Nerdrum felt strongly uncertain about its purpose and outright confused by its aliveness.

"Your consultation is done," the assistant intoned. "If you will just wait in line, we will have you feeling better in no time."

The sick man's rheumatic legs barely obeyed. The people around Gordon Nerdrum, especially the staff, all looked like immoral people: successful, rich, and tatted; crippled by dope, controlled by money and power. It was what happened when identity replaced dignity. He thought they were contemptible, but he did not think he was. He had a legitimate reason for using the drug. He went to church. He had served his country for as long as his disease-ridden body had allowed. His reason was different from whatever reasons they had, and that made it somehow better.

Addicts, Gordon Nerdrum thought. Or maybe he'd said it out loud. He was old, and things like that happened sometimes. The people waiting around him gave him an unwelcoming look.

He was increasingly surprised by just how busy the place was. From what he had seen on the news, it had been busy since they opened for business. In fact, clinics were opening all over British Columbia. Legislation was slow to match the movement, and the clinics were continually raided by the police. *The staff don't seem to care*, the sick man thought, looking around. *They're making plenty of money, and I would imagine most of them probably couldn't find much work anywhere else, having criminal histories.*

What the old man didn't know was that, in their minds, jail wasn't the worst thing. Unemployment was.

Gordon Nerdrum waited his turn; his bloodshot eyes darted impatiently between the posters—posters that read either CURE YOUR OWN CANCER or P IS FOR PANACEA. Depending on which group of letters people in the line shuffled in front of, the first slogan changed from CURE _____ _____ CANCER to ____ YOUR ____ CANCER to just _____ _____ _____ CANCER as he slowly approached the counter.

There was a chart that spun with colour behind the counter. The wheel divided itself into a spectrum of effects that could be read from the centre out or the outside in. The first wheel, at its centre, was segmented into five categories: Neurological, Mental/Behavioural, Gastrointestinal, Pain/Sleep, and Other. He followed the category Pain/Sleep to the next wheel, which abbreviated the serum's biochemical molecules involved. Then there was the outermost wheel, with all the many forms of Pain/Sleep that each molecule of the serum was associated with in the process of recovery: Sleep Apnea, Cramps, Migraines/Headaches, Phantom Limb, Spinal Injury, Fibromyalgia, Insomnia, Pain, Arthritis, Inflammation.

Gordon Nerdrum had found himself in the chart, which must have meant he had come to the right place. And when he looked at the rest of the wheel, it became hard for him to believe that it could do so much.

Once he reached the counter, he gave the prescription to the assistant clerk, and, without saying a word, she turned her back to him only to hastily swirl around again. With her blue-gloved hands, she placed a plastic pouch that resembled a blood bag in front of him. It was transparent and contained various chemical products. Inside was a luminescent viscous liquid, which was yellow, turquoise, orange, or mauve. Globules formed and rose luminously before disappearing. Beside the bag was an apparatus for dispensing the drug through ingestion.

He paid using his military pension fund and was glad to be out of there. It was unnatural for him to have to deal with people he didn't know, and he wished he could have got this another way.

Outside, on the Vancouver street, all the signs were in some Asian language, and all the people were Asian as well. None of them were going into the dispensary. Inside, there had been only black people and white people. This realization fostered the strangest sensation in him, as if he were straddling the boundary between two worlds, and the sensation remained until an unfamiliar pressure on his elbow stopped him.

"Need some help finding your way, sir?" One from the group that suddenly surrounded him, who must have exited the dispensary when Gordon Nerdrum had, was so brazen as to put an arm around his shoulders. Then taking him aside with that same unfamiliar pressure, the round-headed group of grinning Caucasian figures in their heavy army boots and studded, patchwork leather jackets made a ring around him and proceeded to ask him at length—with a sort of feigned courteousness—about his impression of the area, stating that it must have been very different than in his day, culturally, that is.

Gordon Nerdrum felt nothing but the weight of the arms on his shoulders steering him through the army of foreign bodies. A legion of faces and hands, tattooed with vortices of hate, like nebulous spiraling gases. His responses were curt, as he was suddenly in a terrible hurry to get away. Finally, fingers and questions relaxed their grip, and he rushed to find the meter where his vehicle was parked. Fortunately, he wouldn't have to return for ninety days, which was how long the sixty-gram treatment lasted, on average.

•

The area in which the sick man lived was vertical with community apartment buildings, miles from any grounding in historical consciousness. Gordon Nerdrum had lived in many of the buildings. Moved from one to another every couple of years. They had been, after all, built for his generation. Built out of the way of the world's problems. A world that would crush him unsparingly, making him the defenceless prey of juvenile delinquents. He was therefore treated simply as waste, granted only a narrowly limited survival that was as miserable as it was conditional.

He had more and more trouble tolerating the hard and aggressive urban environment. His attitude towards it began to deteriorate, and he felt only bitterness towards immigrants in general. In the most banal way, he had always been racist. He barely knew any other ethnicities and had no wish to become acquainted with them. He only felt a distant and equanimous disdain toward them all. He had neither been unemployed nor threatened by poverty enough to turn his well-bred racist opinions on the ethnic reality into a full-fledged neurosis. And as a regular informer for the security organ, he had destroyed many of these people's lives by handing in written reports to the authorities. These reports were the prelude to an arrest. They served to establish lists of those who were to be classified as a prisoner, who were to be deprived of their passport and the right to vote, who were to be deported to the labour camps, who were never to be released. Having always been able to retreat away from society, where he would play the perfect victim, he simply avoided all contact. *Sticking to one's station in life,* he would say, reassuring himself, *all would be well.*

Gordon Nerdrum lived among old, cluttered, gloomy furnishings. He had thrown out nothing. Everything inanimate—the framed family photos, the military work medals, and the Portuguese rooster souvenir of Barcelos bought during a holiday on the Iberian Peninsula—was being swallowed by time, dissolving into it with the years.

Alone in his study, he examined the objects he had purchased. It took some time for him to fill the dispenser with the drug from the bag. His hands were cumbersome and awkward to work with. The bag was clearly labelled with embossed lettering: "Phoenix Tears."

Onto the tip of his pointer finger, he pushed from the dispenser a single drop of the oily, transparent drug. From out of the round aperture came a bitterish ginger smell. Pleasant, it made Gordon Nerdrum's nostrils flare, and as the substance caught the light, it was somehow translucent, transparent, and opaque all at once. It reminded him of the image of the elongated teardrop on the clinic's computer. However, the drop on his finger seemed less curious than that one, less interested in him than he was in it, and merely sat waiting at the end of his jagged finger. The stubby, head-like appendage of the amoeboid-shaped thing, its glassy surface gleaming with a slightly yellowish tinge, was either aware of him or not—he didn't know.

Before putting the dot onto his tongue, reassuring himself, with only God as his witness, Gordon Nerdrum said: "I never complained. All the pain, all the suffering. It was all my own."

He hadn't complained through all the operations, nor when his family doctor retired and he was put on a waiting list for a new one—one he didn't know and who was far too young, in his opinion—nor when he had to spend all day in a crowded waiting room at a hospital only to be told his turn would come, after the others, his turn would come.

All there was for him was death. He had purchased his plot. He could do nothing with his immobilized body. But life stuck to him as it always had and insisted that everything alive was good.

Gordon Nerdrum licked his crippled finger with a fissured tongue. The drug tasted sickly sweet when it hit his taste buds and either evaporated in an instant or was absorbed. He winced in disgust, more at the idea of it working than at the jellylike texture, which didn't even leave a film in his mouth.

If it could cure him, he would take it. He would take all of it. And he wouldn't complain. No, he would never complain.

2040, November 8

The citizens that were waiting for their turns to cast their ballots occasionally stared at the round heads in front of them. Not a muscle in the faces of the round heads twitched, nor did a sound depart from between their clenched teeth as the angry-faced citizens surrounding them exercised their freedom of speech with intensified ardour. Outspoken citizens jabbed at the emptiness that the round heads' silence gave them and spoke laboriously about a radiant era to come and that which had already passed; they spun tales about stolen funds, sham ventures, and inflated budgets.

The citizens didn't realize they were surrounded by millions of antisocial psychotics: violent lunatics, incurable kleptomaniacs, erotic fetishists, potential murders, maniacs, idiots, and imbeciles. The citizens didn't realize this because there was a reagent that held the round heads constantly in check, held them, that is, in manufactured consent. The round heads had looked like armed detachments when they marched through the streets wrapped in American leather jackets and scraping their heavily worn black boots along the pavement, methodically rapping out two steps a second until they reached the lines of the voting centres.

Parasitized motor nerves insinuated themselves between the will and the muscle of the round heads. As it cycled through their systems, the parasitic substance regulated the round heads' voluntary movements through chemical reactions. Otherwise, the round heads would have attacked the citizens and trampled both them and their culture. That was, of course, set to happen at a later date—after the sixty-fourth quadrennial presidential election.

The round heads, rocking in jerky movements, turned one by one into the voting booths. Slowly and arduously, each of the millions of round heads pushed down on their pencil's lead, inserted between their limp fingers by an overly helpful volunteer, and scrawled unaided the same name on the same line as the round heads in thousands of locations—all within the duration of one electoral night.

After their votes had been cast, the round heads marched straight down the avenues that their voting centres were on, spanning hundreds of roads across the country. They bounced from one dead end to another dead end, banging first into one metal pole and then into another. The round heads, now rounder and reddening, each suddenly experienced a violent conflict between the will of the reagent that was controlling them and that of the round heads themselves.

In their formerly empty hands, each round head quietly filled a bullet case in whatever blind alley they had ended up. Slipping the cartridge into the cylinder of a revolver, each round head cocked the trigger and enfolded the weapon of death in their inert fingers. Their fingers twitched, then gripped the gun handle; the forefinger flexed incorrectly, then adjusted the refractory finger inside the trigger's curve. Each round head's arm sprang up, bent an elbow, and brought the barrel to their own temple. Their facial muscles showed no sign of resistance, their eyelashes fluttered, and the points of their pupils became large black blots.

With their will hardened, they pressed harder and heard a metallic click, then a blast. The human sacks lurched lifelessly forward and slumped to the pavement, dropping dead with a swollen neck and bulging white eyes.

2041, January 20

Augustus Lovejoy was now the chief executive officer, or acting director, of the political party in power. And this, in a sense, made him head propagandist of the altered-right administration. It was his job not only to erase information but also to reconstruct it, and as a political strategist and economic nationalist, he was responsible for a global shift toward nationalism—white nationalism that was both anti-immigration and, until recently, had restricted trade. The embargo was, however, what did all the restricting now.

Obviously, none of this would have anything to do with Biosphere II, but he supposed it was the president who'd have to deal with the fallout, which would be a huge bureaucratic undertaking, and like the religious Saecular Games of ancient Rome, which commemorated the end of one generation with the commencement of another, a celebration of their win was likely to involve its fair share of sacrifices and theatrical performances.

"The second phase of Biosphere II was full of untrained outsiders to academic science. They were crackpots," Augustus Lovejoy said, as he popped out from behind a muddleheaded media scrum, his eyeglasses reflecting the sea of hurrying and jostling human heads. The media were there in response to various allegations, lawsuits, and speculations regarding a member of the second mission. It was said that this person had stolen some kind of invasive species grown illegally within the vivarium.

Under the hollow hum of cobweb telephone wires and the tire-polished asphalt streets of that city-giant, the speaker's voice rose to a dominant level. In the language of official formulas, he proceeded in making it known to the world media that he was in charge of information, that he was at the source of it, and that nothing could happen without his authorization.

"When the Institute of Ecotechnics came to me with this new project for phase three, they seemed so well organized, so inspired, that I simply decided to forget the past. You shouldn't hold the past against anyone. After all, we are all interested in ecological restoration."

The plucked-wire strumming of his voice was a sound that contained no repeated group of words that would fit the sound's accompanying rhythm, and no scale could give them any meaning to the public, much like how the confusion was significant in the notes of an ordered instrument but meant little to untrained ears—an interesting sound that lacked words to describe it.

At the base of the Santa Catalina Mountains, located in Oracle, Arizona, the glass-and-steel-frame facility sat on a sprawling forty acres, at an elevation of four thousand feet above sea level. The aboveground structure was steel tubing and high-performance glass. Its variable volume structures, or "lungs," expanded as the red days heated up the air and contracted in the blue nights' anodyne chill.

Inside the biosphere facility, the ecology developed much like that of an island, with its seven biological biome areas: rainforest, ocean with coral reef, mangrove wetlands, savannah grasslands, fog desert, and two anthropogenic biomes—agricultural systems and a human habitat with living space, laboratories, and workshops.

All of this was formerly owned by Space Biosphere Ventures, whose long-term plan was to gain knowledge about the viability of supporting and maintaining human life in space. Their intent was to use closed biospheres in space colonization. The biospherian crew members who were part of the two-year closed-system expedition were, in a sense, inhabiting a second, fully self-sufficient biosphere—second only to the Earth itself—and aptly named Biosphere II. But during the fifteen-minute breach of the biome, whatever the Institute of Ecotechnics owned became, in the aftermath, an unassailable right of the people.

Eyes-to-the-ground businessman that he was, Augustus Lovejoy, with a briefcase dangling from an apishly long arm and a wide politician smile, wheeled around and stepped into an official state car. The door clapped shut behind him. He had contributed to the falsification of journalism and had done so without a single nervous twitch. He had swallowed his own fictitious poison in order to withstand the public's requests for information. Information reached the public only in completely falsified form because any information that was public was false, and what wasn't public was secret, and what wasn't secret was obscure. Forgeries of history, forgeries of events: pure conspiracy. As was the official report of the biosphere's breach. It was scribbled with lies, mawkishly composed, written and rewritten thousands and thousands of times, revised, copied out, then rewritten again—and Augustus Lovejoy had purposely left out the fact that, before the breach was contained by on-site security, an intruder had taken the undisclosed substance intentionally introduced into the human habitat of the seven biomes.

●

At the breakfast table in the kitchen of his condominium, Augustus Lovejoy was preparing to eat while carefully reading the morning edition of the paper. In one item almost lost within the account of the recent election, he found exactly the kind of neat-and-tidy detail that appealed to his sense of proportion, and he relaxed a little.

Verbs such as "shift," "control," "alter," "command," "optioned," and "function" set him the most at ease. These words were used just as much in the political narrative as on the keyboard of his computer. In fact, Augustus Lovejoy and the altered-right administration functioned much the same as a computer's modifier key, which only modified the action of another key when the two were pressed together. That was exactly how the altered-right party had taken the administration. By themselves, modifier keys did nothing; pressing them alone didn't trigger any action. But when pressed together, they temporarily modified the normal action of any key. People were the same. It was a world of acts, and words had no more influence on acts than anything else.

"A new, epic era of human relations is underway," he said to himself, thinking further ahead to how they could probably have an AI running the economy by reelection. The Chinese and Russian governments already did, and who knows—anything seemed possible. He was about to enjoy his first bite, fork to open mouth and coffee cup in hand, when his phone rang.

"How did you get this number? This is a private line," he said, ready to hang up the moment he heard the unfavourable introduction.

"It's my job to get numbers like yours. I'd like to ask you several questions concerning your involvement in the sixty-fourth presidential election."

He was still on the line. Usually it would have been over by now; he would have hung up. But things were not as they usually were, and he was feeling as though it was time to release information to the public. His party was in power. They were in office. Loyalties had shifted. He was safe. He liked this.

"Are you involved in the testing of psychochemical agents on human subjects?" the woman asked. Augustus Lovejoy bristled at her effort to shine a light on his past business ventures.

Thresholds and liability—what was acceptable and who was responsible—that was all that mattered to journalists.

"If you are referring to Biosphere II, then no," he said, in his ruthless but thoroughly open American manner. "It was a space simulator, and I no longer have an active role with them."

"The Eastern Alliance has placed an embargo on trade with the West because of genetically contaminated grain. How will the altered-right government respond to this?"

"Our government has already formed the USENA to mitigate any effects the embargo may have on the European-American economy."

"You mean the labor camps that have been popping up in Canada and where the Mediterranean used to be."

Augustus Lovejoy let out a gigantic snort—one of contempt, of disbelief. "You think that just because you've read the reports you know something," he said, without irony.

She wasn't finished. "How is the ethnic-resettlement program going to solve the immigration problem?"

"The Mars settlement is a proposed reparation project for those who have become dispossessed by climate change and political instability in their own countries and are seeking out asylum wherever it is made available."

"But there is no Mars colony, is there? Just another temporary place to send people who have been reduced to speaking bodies. I'm sure the consent form waived both social ethics and individual morality."

Again, he toted out the official government line: "You've got our reports."

She paused. He knew she was frowning. The reports had been reclassified since the election—all of this was now speculation.

"I've got nothing to say to you, then," he said gruffly, in warning. "No further explanation. Nothing."

"Does the incidence of infection through the use of the psychotropic drug Phoenix Tears have anything to do with the break-in at Biosphere II by a suspected domestic terrorist who goes by the name of Johannes Van Vyferyken?"

Silence is the best response.

He hung up.

Augustus Lovejoy pulled a section out of the paper, placed it in front of him on the table, and consumed the text posthaste, without reflecting or delegating. Along the rough and dirty paper, the brown-grey letters rushed. When he found what he was looking for, he shoved a finger between the sloppily printed words and, tugging impatiently at the raggedy page, tore the pages he had leafed through apart; taking these pages with him as he pushed away from the table and got up, scraping the chair against the floor as he did so. Augustus Lovejoy paced the length of the room with not only the ferocity of a caged predator, but also the brutal hatred of a trapped animal who is forced to share its cage with other creatures.

He hadn't missed anything, not really. The article made no connection between the drug and the government. Just stated that Biosphere II had been demolished and the land sold to a real estate company. No mention of the third mission at all. It said something about how the facility should have been donated to the University of Arizona, but that was nothing.

She was just attempting to get a different version, he thought. *But there will be more of that to come, more who will accuse me and the administration of much worse.*

No one imagined that there was always another by his side. The real him. They always thought him identical to himself.

He wore a human mask in order to lie. No one recognized him beneath that mask of equality, nor did they guess that it was a mask, because no one knew masked players existed in this world. He wore that human mask, the mask that was a lie, and yet he was entirely his own mask: that impersonal, inexpressive, and indifferent mask whose fierce function was not originally a human function but that, out of practical necessity, became human. It was through this lie that he had found himself within an even greater lie, an entire political system of liars, and it pained him not to speak openly about these beliefs in his speeches. About the power of a lie. He secretly wanted it to happen. But that would have been a difficult speech, and he was not upset to be spared from ever having to give it.

It was the people of America who had fucked up. For a climber like Augustus Lovejoy, power meant he could do what he wanted. He wanted to climb, and they had let him: from the Pentagon to Wall Street to Hollywood to Biosphere II to the White House. They had let him play musical chairs in rooms he shouldn't have been allowed into well before he had joined the altered-right administration.

The peoples' mistake was a naive mistake. A mistake that divided them into an "us" and a "them." The critical difference being that the naive believed in the pure American dream, which had no connection, no point of contact, with reality; the vetted government bigwigs and the like believed in the imperfect dream, with its roots thoroughly at home in reality. This division gave rise to ever more clear-cut, simple-minded, brutal logic, a bewitchingly crude guiding principle based on the sacredness of trillions and trillions of facts and those who mediate them.

Yet now Augustus Lovejoy was the one who could not escape the past they had given him, even if he wanted to. Whatever he felt or thought or said in the present was nothing more than an echo from that past. Even after all the amputations—the thousand amputations, the scars, the hollowing out—that came with changing oneself as many times as he had in recent years, he remained as much his past as everybody else was theirs.

The people of America would not let him obliterate himself. Not entirely. They would not let him disappear. Instead, they wanted to see more of him. It was the only power they still had over him. And that was why he needed to shift the focus to

Johannes Van Vyferyken—so he could shed his past, sweep away the memory of it. Augustus Lovejoy needed to make the man an extreme fundamentalist of the altered-left to balance things out again. After all, he didn't make a problem if he didn't have a solution—that was just not American.

It was going to be simple as pie, as they say. Johannes Van Vyferyken had sent a letter to all the major transnational newspapers indicating that he would desist from any and all terrorist activities if they printed his essay. The newspapers informed the police, and the police the government, which was probably how the journalist over the phone had known what name to use with him. Augustus Lovejoy would just let them print the soon-to-be-famous piece in the semiofficial government papers, on the next-to-last page, with the sporting results and stock market reports. Then, the transnational papers would be sure to follow suit, and Johannes Van Vyferyken's guilt would become so widespread that it would reverse from fiction to fact.

The manifesto was typical of hair-brained political treatises: a protestation of one's own faith. Augustus Lovejoy had skimmed over it with his AI wrist console vehemently at first and then again more conscientiously—it was depressing so it had to be true. For not only was it really long, but it also banged on the same point about "agrilogistics" ad nauseam. Its thesis was that agrilogistics, the agricultural program that had been running for twelve thousand years, was a survival paradox: in attempting to survive at any cost, humanity had caused mass extinction and generated global warming and murder-suicides. Capitalism was changing but it still ran by this implicit logic. And it was all because hominids had stopped hunting and gathering and started farming grain. Because they had settled down despite their contradictory nature.

The headline Augustus Lovejoy pictured rang true: "Crazy mountain man goes on rampage because society too problematic." It would nicely deflect attention from the government's involvement with Johannes Van Vyferyken in orchestrating the genetic contamination. A classic antihero, like Dostoevsky's Unabomber, Raskolnikov. Both published notorious essays and both were either evil or sick to their core. Intelligent but cruel. That traditional villain essential to any fantastic narrative. The masses would conveniently replace his personality with this cardboard cutout.

You're worse than the bacteria: they eat facts, you eat the facts' meaning, Augustus Lovejoy thought about himself. He found himself wanting to put the two individual terms, "fact" and "eater," closer together. Through their linguistic blend of sound and meaning, he created a new entity, a new expression, a portmanteau that somehow more than accurately described what people were being made into. *Facteaters.*

What Augustus Lovejoy was afraid of now was looking out of the window of his decently private condominium and seeing the infected walking along the sidewalk—not just one but many of them. The marching of morbid, millennial things. People in all the cities of America were already wearing sickness masks. He decided not to look, just to be on the safe side. At least not for a while. Instead, he concentrated on his breakfast, which had become cold and tasteless.

What those people in safety masks didn't understand was that it was the food that was infected. Grains, mostly, and the animals that ate the grains. *Like a really bad gluten intolerance.* He laughed malignantly and ate. His food was harmless. Lab grown. Only the public food supply was genetically contaminated by the parasitic fungus. He had made sure of that. So long as the millions of madnesses didn't break through to him, he'd be all right with it. And as trivial a task as it was to think about these things as he ate, at least it was a familiar event. It helped restore his sense of the regularity of these repugnant realities.

Gordon Nerdrum was a sick man. He continued to sit in the unlit room of his community apartment house until he was finished his ninety-day treatment. The chemical pouch was becoming flaccid and slowly grew flat; it was nearly empty. There was only its smell now, increasingly pungent and spicy, which made his head spin, confused his fingers, and caused his knees to tremble slightly. The pain and the swelling of his joints was, if not cured, at least temporarily mitigated.

He had been experiencing what he assumed was a nocebo effect of taking the medicine. After each dosage, a black sleep instantly descended on him from above, and both syringe and man became empty. When he woke, a nearly inaudible voice began to whisper and cut into Gordon Nerdrum's thoughts. It warned him of things, seemed to have the unsettling ability to see the future. Told him who, in the building of senior citizens, would die next and who would move into the dead tenant's apartment house. To Gordon Nerdrum's astonishment, the voice had been right on more than one occasion.

In the dark, receding corners of the low-ceilinged, coffin-shaped room, an emaciated thing, the shapeless thing that the voice belonged to, waited silently. It had told him that it was allergic to light and preferred a damp, dark room. And so Gordon Nerdrum kept the lights low and left the shower running, without the fan.

"Gordon," the mouthless thing said. "Gordon, tell me about your late wife. How did she die? Of course, I already know. I read your thoughts. But I'd like to hear it from you."

Gordon Nerdrum, initially reluctant to answer, eventually thought better of it—the thing would pester him if he did not.

"She had dementia. She forgot how to live. I recognized some of the warning signs at Christmas. It went from mild to moderate to severe: memory loss, movement, hoarding, mood swings, difficulty with new environments, loss of language. And then the major motor control declined"—he paused—"along with everything else. I guess it ran in her family, in their genes. It happened very quickly. Actually, we always thought I would go first. Seeing as I was always the one with all the complications."

This was true. He never thought he would outlive his wife. She used to joke cruelly about him leaving her to die alone, and he would pick his teeth and she would complain about that, too. He was the one who was alone now. *How the tables have turned*, he thought, with a kind of guilty enjoyment and a woebegone grin across his face.

"Oh, Gordon. How dreadful for you. Yes, the weak have a special gift when it comes to suffering. Isn't that true, Gordon? You could even go as far as to say you have a special talent for it. Suffering, that is." It sounded as if there was a smirk in what the mouthless thing had said. But the voice and the mouth were both in his head.

"Do you know what I am, Gordon?"

"A hallucination?"

"In a way, yes. But that does not make me any less real than, let's say, your dead wife. I am, in a sense, the sickness that was inside of you all these very many years. Living in your rotting bones."

Gordon Nerdrum did not speak. The organic entity had sprung directly from a hallucinatory vision. It had oozed out of him, dragging its shapeless form along the big one-bedroom apartment. He sat in deathlike repose, vacantly looking in the opposite direction.

He and his wife were particularly old-fashion. Dressed in their rigid, rather grim clothes, accustomed to repressing their emotions and desires, the couple may have at times succeeded in forgetting their connection to the impurities of life. If it wasn't for this wife's psychosis, which proved to be an absolutely impossible task for them, as it went far beyond what was acceptable within their puritanical social circle. It seemed self-evident to him that people with pure Anglo-Saxon origin were by nature entitled to the highest privileges within the social order. Valuing orderly, traditional notions over freer, progressive ones. Of course, these beliefs would all fall apart after a minor event in the modern world, suicidal depression combined with a small bottle of sleeping pills, with considerable consequences, attempted mariticide with the sharpest knife in the kitchen. Their best-case scenario, eternal life, was off the table.

"It's nice to finally talk, isn't it? And you are feeling much better, now that I am here and not in there?" Its questions remained rhetorical, and Gordon Nerdrum imagined a shadowy arm pointing in his direction.

The sound of movement came from the corner. A soft, wet movement that crept close to where his eyes were fixed. Into his nostrils drifted the smell of rot. And then, there it was. Looking down the length of his long and fleshless nose, he saw a yellowish, organic thing silently flow and gather itself together into a heap of small globes that comprised its physical being. The slime mould pulsed.

Then, with purpose, it slid under the door to the hotbed of the bathroom, out of sight, leaving only a trail of slime residue behind.

65

"One riddle over another," Jaegwon Choy shouted, a wizened finger straightened up like an exclamation mark, as if to banish all supernatural explanations from the classroom. He wanted his students to understand that the mind was a natural phenomenon and so seeking it required a naturalistic explanation.

"Professor Choy," a student said, "if one event occurs, could it have occurred in the same manner if it happened to another person? Could it occur in the same manner if it had occurred at a different time?"

The student who had asked this question had a habit of looking up the strong arguments against his theory and then voicing them, accompanied by an audience.

"No—neither are true," Jaegwon Choy said. "Because different conditions would lead to separate events. The event itself is the centre of being: the body-mind of the person absorbs the event only by being absorbed by it.

"Being absorbed by an event is what we are all doing, all the time. Absorbing the generic events of our lives by being absorbed by them."

The same student interrupted the professor again.

"Shouldn't the event include both the span of time of the event and the area in which it occurs? A spatiotemporal region, I mean."

Like a flash of lightning includes both the span of time of the flash of lightning and the area in which it occurs. Jaegwon Choy paused. *Or like the West. The West constitutes a spatiotemporal region, since the embargo, anyway—the Eastern Alliance and their restriction on trade is the flash.*

After class, Jaegwon Choy returned to his office, where everyone visited him, but not for anything important. Not anymore. He left his door open anyway.

Retired but allowed to retain his title, an emeritus at Brown University, he was significantly less known than his more infamous contemporaries. He looked up his name on the university's website. It hadn't yet been removed from the online faculty list, nor had the short description that summarized his existence there: a Korean-American philosopher and schizoanalyst who spoke French.

He was, among the academics who were supposed to be his equals, a skewed percentile of diversity. Yes, like them, he was upper-middle class, had a title of distinction, and was of a widely accepted cosmopolitan ethnicity, but that also meant he often had to take a side that went against his best interests, especially as of late. Had to accept invitations to professional feastings of haute cuisine created by French molecular gastronomy engineers and other social events under the pretense that he represented a kind of bohemian thought. It was almost an inverse relationship or a negative correspondence: he understood their privilege only as much as they fetishized his suffering. Both moved in opposite directions the more one knew about the other. The *other* was just code for him and people like him, and so Plato's category of the other only ever deferred the problem instead of solving it.

"Praxis," they told him, humming over a starter of jelly balls that tasted like apple and lemon, an entirely synthetic gourmet dish, "what we do with ourselves in our world, is all anyone has." And they weren't wrong about this. They just weren't right. He wanted to tell them that *different* wasn't always dangerous, even though most of the time it was. Instead, he would usually cross his eyes in dismay and surprise them with an unexpected thought like, "Then I'll have to pull you out of your solipsism." They enjoyed the occasional scare in his best white-speak. Besides, he seemed like the type of intellectual one never had any trouble from. At just the right moment, their lunch of smooth, crusty and frosty lobster fricassée would be served with polyphenol sauce (made with tartaric acid, glucose and polyphenols). He was constantly aware of the aura of tension around these academicians and would have continued to frown at his side of plain vegetables, maybe the carrots, or just the molecules that made up those carrots (carotenoids, pectins, fructose and glucuronic acid). Rubbing their hands together, they'd have dug into their grated carrots first thing; and he'd copy them.

In this American life of his, Jaegwon Choy was resigned to accept that neither his time nor his place was right. Human time was thinking, and he often caught himself spending that human time thinking with hands clenched and arms clasped high behind his back in a kind of self-resistance. As long as the aggression shown toward easterners since the embargo didn't take a turn for the worse—a daily thought that admittedly caused him grief because it meant his possible death—he wouldn't have to worry about the troubles he might encounter in his next life, someplace else. He hoped the American public would continue to accept this political sanction without demur.

However, there was certainly a degree of demur, if only a show of reluctance or hesitance over the sanction, a process of objections and raised doubts, some disorganized protesting over all the delays and deferrals concerning accessible food security. Nothing more. Nothing violent had happened to him yet.

●

Jaegwon Choy still taught, still interviewed, still wrote influential articles, thinking all the while that retirement was not the retirement of thought. In general, his intellectual life was at a standstill. He was making some progress on what was likely to be no more than a simple compliment to the major work he had already done in his field, but he still couldn't seem to write. His interest in the life of the mind had diminished to the disfavour, on the other hand, of his social life, and still on the other, the life of his body, which was to become considerably more important. All in all, he was endlessly tormented by some dull, numb pain, ache or affliction, never leaving him enough peace to make clear-eyed conclusions about anything.

As for his retirement, he was off to a bad start. He had trouble giving up his professional and intellectual responsibilities. It was a universe of privilege. The new people at the head of the institute had even promised that nothing would interfere with his real work if he stayed on. No hard classes nor any dissertations to advise. Mostly just a few undergraduate lectures.

There was something different about the society he lived in, and he spent more and more of his days trying to figure out exactly what that was. It wasn't just the neo-fascist films coming out of Hollywood since the altered-right took government; these mostly just pushed the usual American exceptionalism and denied global warming through ridiculous analogies such as rightist politicians being locked in a Turkish bathhouse in Brussels by leftist radicals until they overheated.

Maybe it was that today there was no clearly defined alternative, that this deadlock prevented a thinker from thinking to the end of any predicament. It was hard to see, as if he were looking through fog. *Maybe*, he thought, *the future has come quicker than expected, like the headlights of an oncoming train at a flag stop.*

Jaegwon Choy had always felt that he and his theories would be best understood in the future. Maybe it was because the English language didn't have a morphological future tense. There were no verb structures specific to the tense. He felt that even "will"—as in, "We will make America (input adjective)"—had no futurity in it. The

English language was, ultimately, mired in the past and present tense. History for English speakers involved choosing to include or exclude the politically problematic programs of their past in the present. But it wasn't history they were dealing with in the future, if the future was a history at all; it was a history of evolution, and evolution was up to chance.

Of course, the communists had always liked his theories. They found them useful in justifying things like the altered-left. Communistic kitschy art was gradually replacing the silently racist paintings of white men that lined the university's walls. Although Jaegwon Choy didn't mind his thinking being applied to certain social movements, he didn't particularly like it being applied to communism. It seemed un-American, and he was un-American enough as it was. He preferred the natural sciences.

He looked out of his office's large rectangular window. On the roof was the blue-tiled courtyard of an urban garden for students in the natural sciences. Jaegwon Choy, driven to despair by the embargo's banana shortage, had decided to help build a glass hothouse on the roof and plant a banana sapling or two.

On overcast days, such as this one, and at night, when he spent long hours working on his theory, the greenhouse glowed. It glowed, and the glass panels made the incandescent lights, emanating from within, seem more golden than they actually were. A tropical twilight of yellow chandeliers.

Occasionally, Jaegwon Choy would catch a student standing in the courtyard holding one of the biggest of the bananas so that it protruded out of the fly of his pants—the student would stroke it with his other hand, the great jaundiced fruit curved toward the sky.

The garden didn't produce much, running primarily off the goodwill of volunteers and students. But there was always a plentitude of bananas: radiant yellow and humid green. Jaegwon Choy visited the greenhouse regularly, if only to get a giant banana cluster for Banana Breakfast. He made everything with them in the staff kitchenette, and when he was cooking, he would allow the fragile, flowery, permeating, surprising fragrance to meander among the offices and down the halls and stairwells of the building's philosophy wing.

He would make banana omelettes, banana sandwiches, banana casseroles, mashed bananas moulded into the shape of an American eagle, bananas blended with eggs into batter for French toast, bananas squeezed out of a pastry nozzle across the quivering creamy reaches of a banana blancmange. Tall cruets of pale banana syrup to ooze over banana waffles. A giant glazed crock where diced bananas had been fermenting since summer with wild honey. Muscat raisins dipped into foaming mugs full of banana mead. Banana croissants and banana kreplach, and banana oatmeal and banana jam and banana bread, and bananas flamed in aged brandy. And on occasion, if he had reason to celebrate progress in his theory, a *bananes glacée* or a banana frappé with crushed ice.

Admittedly, retirement had something to do with his inspired activities in the kitchen. He tried to bleed time in other ways: volunteering and writing poetry and growing his hair out and reading jaded fashion magazines on the Internet and playing with the pair of adopted sister kittens his two daughters had given him before they went overseas for work in Korea. He was proud that they were making good use of their educations, but the cats were obvious replacements for what he had lost.

His daughters had insisted that the sister kittens would be psychologically good for him right now. "Practice self-care," they had said, and he believed them despite himself. By "right now" they were probably referring to the situation with their mother, his ex-wife, who had gone through what she had called a "lifequake" and started seeing other people. His daughters had seen it coming, of course, and so the cats made sense. And in a way so did the rest. Well, maybe not the bananas.

But underneath all his restless activity, Jaegwon Choy was waiting. Waiting for just the right moment to blow the whistle on everything that was happening in America. The evidence was available to him; he only needed the heroism to follow through with it.

●

Heroism is having faith in disbelief. To no longer believe in believing the beliefs that we do not have but nevertheless say that we have requires a certain kind of faith, Jaegwon Choy thought. *Thinking through the hopelessness because courage is thought, and thought is the greatest of all actions.*

As if he were a Dresden spy, Jaegwon Choy had received the instructions anonymously for years and then didn't. He still had the AI wrist console. It was now locked away in a safety deposit box with an outdated cell phone and the key to a room on the second storey of an abandoned office building that seemed to be forever under construction. It was his own concrete biome. The only door in his life that he constantly kept closed.

After giving a brief talk on the surveillance of the few by the many, known in his field as Synopticon, at an international IT governance conference in Halifax, Nova Scotia, Jaegwon Choy had been approached by a nondescript type, a person he couldn't immediately place because nothing about that person stood out, wanting to outsource information from him.

"What kind of information?" Jaegwon Choy asked, as equally noncommittal as the nondescript had been with him but nonetheless curious about what she had to say.

At this point both had switched off their AI wrist consoles and were standing on the outside balcony of the hotel lounge. "You would be working completely outside the AI networks, so never use your own AI wrist console. There is only one privately secured system we're interested in exploring."

The nondescript was brief and hardly showed any sign that she was talking with Jaegwon Choy. Her shiny hair had the look of some kind of cold, hard plastic, and her industrial, nyloned legs moved with the uncanny lag of things requiring an external command. The leg-parts had an elsewhere quality to them that, like the total person, he had a difficult time describing for himself. *Too many parts and too small a sum.*

Hesitant initially, Jaegwon Choy had agreed to help. The old Machiavellian adage "The enemy of my enemy is my friend" made it easier for him to do so. Not that he had entirely defined for himself who that enemy or even who that friend would be, but it wasn't often that he could put schizoanalysis to practical use.

He was told that contact would be made after the conference by an anonymous caller at an undisclosed time on the cell phone the woman had provided for him. When the call finally came through, the speaker's voice was masked by a filter and seemed more like artificial general intelligence than genuine human speech, which made him immediately second-guess what he was getting involved in.

Jaegwon Choy wished he could have confirmed it through a test of some sort—a Turing, Wozniak, Goertzel, Nilsson, Severyns or whatever other test was currently being used to prove human-level AGI. He often thought his students were automatons of one kind or another, and got them to make him an average mug of American coffee, the Wozniak test, to prove they weren't. Or was it that he wanted to prove that they were? He couldn't remember the objective and what the results meant. If they could obtain a degree or perform at least as well as a human in an economically important job or correctly assemble flat-packed furniture, which he could hardly do himself, that had to mean they were human.

Since the nondescript at the conference had been a female and of no particular ethnicity, or just mixed ethnicity, Jaegwon Choy guessed that she was a gynoid. Everyone was at least a low-bandwidth cyborg, anyway, when using their AI wrist consoles, and although the West was in a sort of AI winter itself, the sudden and unexpected intelligence explosions in the East were comparable to an AI spring. Something to be worried about, if not frightened of. Frightened that the intelligence explosion was an evocation, a summoning of the demons. Was the gynoid a Chinese security strategy? An example of large-scale surveillance over other sovereign states through doctored technologies?

Next, an AI wrist console had arrived through the mail. It hadn't been cleaned of its information, and had previously belonged to a person named Augustus Lovejoy. As a console, it would have also had an operator—an AI operator—and would have been used to maintain, monitor, and control the status of some system or network it had originally been in connection with.

Jaegwon Choy still made regular trips to the safety deposit box, wondering if they had tried to reach him since the last time he checked. They never had. Disappointed, he thought about destroying the evidence but decided that it would be better to have it and not need it than to need it and not have it.

He looked at the black-spotted fruit, which he'd let ripen in his office, and thought about those five years and how they had ceased to exist, covered up as they were by the ruling government. Sworn to secrecy.

Looking down at the day's lesson plan from his curriculum, his thoughts of the items in the safety deposit box continued, and so he philosophized on these items, as he thought of and philosophized on everything else—that is, he considered it an Event.

•

In the kitchenette, which had become his bananary since retirement, Jaegwon Choy chopped several bananas into pieces. Brewed coffee. Pureed the 'nanas in milk and cracked golf-ball-shaped eggs. Blended the blonde mash of fruit into a waffle batter, not too vigorously, with a wire whisk. Minced with a nervous blade. Put in a bit of butter and melted it in the skillet. Peeled more bananas, sliced them lengthwise, and sizzled the long slices in the butter. Upended peels lay scattered everywhere. At this point, the odour pervading the building had likely gotten his colleagues drooling, and they had to know very well that Jaegwon Choy never had much of an appetite after one of his cooking sprees and that this meant forkfuls of delicious, warm, gooey food in their stomachs.

"A whole way of life lies before me," one remarked with a laugh, gulping down the fusion food that looked American but tasted Korean.

And there it was, Jaegwon Choy's "way of life." He heard this a lot. Cynicism wasn't an Eastern worldview. The insanity of cynicism was, according to him, what people needed to be saved from. More importantly, Western questions necessitated Western answers. But when it came to cultural difference, he was cynical about what was or wasn't racist. *We do this and they do that. It's relative. Universal]. Equivalent.*

"Without America's efforts in the two world wars," another of them said, undoing the top button of their pants to make more room, "democracy would have collapsed. And without democracy, there would be no peace, no way of life enjoyed between democracies. There would be a Third World War."

Jaegwon Choy thought of the colours at the festivals—weddings and processions, funerals and holidays—the colours of the food, the colours of the clothing, the colours of the music, the colours of the culture. *All reminders of what the modern world could have lost without America's efforts. The American way of life is everyone's way of life. Except.*

"Except that America's economic success after the war was a fluke. And there's no proof that says the American economy will stay that way forever."

Somebody who hadn't touched the food made a skeptical noise at this remark, and so the speaker, a black man who, from what Jaegwon Choy could already tell by his opinion on the matter, was probably a postmodern neo-Marxist of some sort, went on to explain. "The recessional conditions are an outcome of trying to force an unrepeatable historical accident, an anomaly, into a natural law of economics. But the only law transnationals ever discovered was to cheapen and so undervalue what we weren't willing to lose: labour-power, food, energy, and raw materials. And since nobody votes for our capitalist leaders, cheap nature remains law. It's the opposite of exceptionalism; it's anti-exceptionalism."

The colours were there because of the suffering. *And before the enjoyment it was because we suffered that we had culture.* These exceptional people, Americans like Jaegwon Choy considered himself to be, reminded him of the colour they had all escaped from. Any chance at real culture was gone for them. Did that mean it was gone for him, too?

Each problem cried in its own language. Hangul was the most scientific system of writing in any country. The world's best alphabet. It's correlation between spelling and pronunciation was the highest. And yet, the world did not speak Hangul.

Japanese colonists and then post-colonialist Korean nationalists had given Koreans *han,* but what did Americanization give to his Korean uniqueness? A sort of second-generational *han,* maybe, but if there was no English equivalent, could there be such a state of mind or soul? Combined: *han* was a feeling of unresolved resentment as a result of injustices suffered, a sense of helplessness because of the overwhelming odds against one, a feeling of acute pain, an obstinate urge to take revenge and to right the wrong. Both sadness and hope. Hatred or regret. Shared suffering. Beauty of sorrow. Beauty of health. Beauty of naturalness. Beauty of unity.

They do this and we do not do that. It's not relative. Un-universal. Nonequivalent.

•

Back in his office, having left the fruits of his labour to those young professors and assistants still in their hungry years, Jaegwon Choy began reading the little symbols of a student's thesis that had the waffle marks of a shoe on it. He began by checking the student's logical argument, leaving his strange, insect-like writing in the margins of the paper as he did so.

In his class, he taught that an event could be defined and theorized because it was structured, composed of three things:

1. Object(s), [x],

2. A property, [P], and

3. Time or a temporal interval, [t].

Events are then defined using the operation [x, P, t], he reasoned. Next, a unique event as opposed to a generic one, like cooking the bananas he took from the greenhouse, was defined by two principles:

a) The existence condition, and

b) The identity condition.

From this, he taught his students to use the event's previously defined composition and principles to further define events under five conditions:

1. They are unrepeatable, unchangeable particulars that include changes and the states and conditions of that event.

2. They have a semi-temporal location.

3. Only their constructive property creates distinct events.

4. Holding a constructive property as a generic event creates a type-token relationship between events.

5. Events are not limited to their four requirements.

He needed to consider Ole Fogh Kirkeby's take on things, only recently translated into English, for the fifth condition, to make sense of the unique event: if a banana does not meet any of the conditions and principles that define it as a generic banana, it is possible, according to the fifth condition, that it may be something that resembles a banana while not actually being a banana, such as a new species that will eventually become generic itself. Ole Fogh Kirkeby used the Danish word *begivenheden* for the unique event, which seemed to capture this fifth condition nicely, as it focused on the way that humans are "evented." But, still, Jaegwon Choy did not think it was likely that generic events could be picked out from unique events, whether the theory was a common-sense theory of the behaviour of middle-sized objects or a highly sophisticated physical theory. *Events were*, he thought, *just too much for even the best scientific theories to relativize.*

He stopped scribbling on the student's thesis. Realizing just how difficult it was trying to explain himself to this student, he sat back in his chair, which creaked out a groan. Like everyone, the student was either not an idiot or was an idiot. There was no third option.

Jaegwon Choy was clearly the idiot, and he stared through a smile at this admission: the layers of memory that encompassed his and his idea's history had been compressed together, as onto a single plane, for so long that it was really more of a feeling than a conscious thought for him. His mind had unquestionably slowed its pace, and although he was allowed to teach his class and keep his office and title, he was not the thinker he once was. It was harder for him to push further than what he had achieved in his youth. The attention required for abstraction was noticeably diminishing, as if his brain were once again reverting to its pre-abstract-thinking conditions. The skin covering his cranium and his idea became a bit wrinkled in places, and closer to the bone.

However, he also had a renewed appreciation for his younger self, the person he had once been and would never be again. The person who had sat on panels with Alain Badiou and was the only Asiatic-American student of Gilles Deleuze. He who had taken to the boulevards with Foucault to protest the increasing presence of a police state in France and was not only present for the beginning of postmodernism but swore to seek it out to its seemingly meaningless end. In love and anxiety.

It was 2042, nearly eighty years since that beginning, and that meant he was almost one hundred years old. Ending his own aging through negligible senescence treatments kept him suspended in what was beginning to feel like a permanent midlife crisis. He didn't look a day over sixty. So all those infamous thinkers had gone through the usual pro-aging trance and died, and he lived. They were immortalized by their mortality, while he was demoralized by his indeterminate life span.

But who gets to be immortal? Doesn't everyone deserve to die sometime? He wondered above all whether substitute immortality could even be brought to a halt—before concluding no.

Those with longevity treatments were bound to not only make it more difficult for any new ideas to ever enter the universities but also contributed to the formation of a self-deifying class system in which immortality dictated through superior biology. Which was why he was retiring. Those with reduced life spans, on the other hand, sought out more extreme psychological compensation for their position in the nascent class system through mystical networks and drug-induced chemical moods. Many of his students had become like this, what he called "pulp": a soft, shapeless mass of material. Utterly schizoidal.

Relying on the massive and unending impact of immigrant populations, immigration held out the hope of a new age of enlightenment for the Western world. There was even an Asian-American rumoured to be campaigning for the next US presidency. But here, again, scientific and technological progress had allowed politicians to take the plunge and strategically gain back the minority vote via post-racial reconstructive surgeries. He was feeling as though society was on the threshold, or perhaps the first phases in a rise towards the systematic dismantling of identity politics. Because the popular wrath of the public had proven to be a big dangerous animal, with voting behaviours that could annihilate the stability of a country over a single term, politicians were now desperately trying to create an artificial mankind, whose mass submissiveness only thought in terms of election cycles.

Was it then absurd, a sign of an increasing senility despite the longevity treatments, perhaps, that he thought the source of the current political situation, the embargo, was caused by what was in that safety deposit box? And, although he couldn't further elaborate on his theory, wasn't it the first premise when identifying an event to point out that it has a clear beginning and end? Wasn't the decline of the West the end of one event and the rise of the East the beginning of another?

●

The AI wrist console in the safety deposit box had never been analyzed by anything but the AI operator it was synchronized with, and so the information on it was inaccessible to anyone besides its owner, Augustus Lovejoy. On it was a comprehensive assemblage of scientific papers and other findings from Biosphere II.

The scientific papers ranged from calibrated models that described the system's metabolism, hydrologic balance, and heat and humidity to papers that described the development of the rainforest, mangrove, ocean, and agronomic systems in the biome's carbon-dioxide-rich environment to video logs of the biospherians themselves.

There was one researcher, among the audio and visual documents in his possession, that he had considered with the most maniacal precision. Céline Høltermand (this, the internet informed him) had almost mythical status amongst contemplative fans of her radical, experimental essays, partly because of their visionary and disturbing depiction of the mental state of schizophrenic brain parasitism, and also because of her recent invisibility. He could only find one talk attached to the name that had resurfaced from the dark recesses of the web on various video streaming platforms. It was her last known public appearance. She was virtually impossible to locate; some speculated that she had committed suicide later that same year, but no confirmation of this was ever made. Certain people, the majority intellectuals, were being erased, deleted forever, there remained no trace of them, and it was as if they had never existed.

Nothing in her hypothesis explained what it was that allowed these hallucinations to escape the unusual limitations of the cognitive functions. There couldn't possibly be a bifurcation of non-observable phenomena appearing at the same time as certain observable events. However, denying a given observer's own mental projections access to a non-provable substantial sequence of events did not necessarily render them incompatible with the global evolution of a form through the common consciousness or progressive interconnection of cognitive and memory processors.

In fact, according to other interpretations, some of these hallucinations were of a different order from those experienced by individuals; of artificial origin, they were perhaps the spontaneous production of cognitive schizophrenia. Mental half-dreams were propagating themselves through transmission channels opened by a brain parasite (disease X) whose primary devices for biochemical surveillance were generated through the production of a series of psychoactive waves that exerted control over these branching channels of reality, cabling consciousnesses together to better create and organize power structures.

From this congeries of bewitched objects, Jaegwon Choy was able to reconstruct the biosphere's *supervenience*—a term he had coined in his youth and that described how a system's upper-level properties (like climate change) could be determined by its lower-level properties (human activity)—a phenomenon which created a relation between the biospherians that had seemingly destroyed all oppositions. There, life and death did not oppose one another. Neither did love oppose indifference. No, nothing was as it had been, and everything was totally original. Everything was a unique occurrence.

He saw the biospherians put themselves in the mind of an owl or a whale or a bumblebee or something that didn't even have a mind. He saw the human transform into the nonhuman. And, as if all this had occurred in a gigantic Petri dish, the breach that was the Event contained in Biosphere II, together with the biospherians, had become "events" out here. The events that carried the radically new oppositions from that Petri-dish world to this larger one, were now quickly becoming a philosophical Event—with a capital "E"—unto themselves.

Now, having tied the knot of the argument, Jaegwon Choy pulled and the strings came together by means of their meaning. *The Event is a multiple that basically does not make sense according to the rules of the "situation"; in other words, it does not make sense according to the rules of existence. Hence, the Event "is not," and therefore, in order for there to be an Event, there must be an "intervention" that changes the rules of the situation to allow that particular Event to be. The breach changed the rules. The breach intervened. As God did with Abraham.*

And this was how the government had acted toward the expedition, as if the Event "was not," as if the rules that counted toward its existence did not count. When, in fact, they did. More and more, they, whatever the empty signifier "they" stood for, were becoming the new order of things.

The new order would replace him and everyone else with the rules of its situation, and despite Biosphere II's proximity to the Earth, it was distinctly unearthly, containing things that one could have guessed developed in the farthest reaches of the universe. Or the next. Things emerging from the physical but that were not themselves physical. Things that made him believe that although most mental properties were reducible, some, or at least those in Biosphere II, were not.

Then again, Jaegwon Choy was never one to recognize events as they were unfolding; every time they came to a head, they surprised him like the explosion of instances that they were. *Every Event has a moment-by-moment structure*, he thought. *A structure that is beyond measurement or comprehension—one that is too complex to have an image, visible only if time has slowed down through thought to the point that we see the world as indifferent equations and so arrive at a perfect universal conclusion, composed of individual intentions and a result of unconscious choices. Chance and choosing. Chance and choosing are just what might have happened anyway.*

He thought this over solemnly as he picked up an overripe banana, brittle and blackish, which was, surprisingly, not attracting any fruit flies, and began to peel off its organic wrapper. But under the skin was not the soft and sweet potassium-rich centre one might have expected. Just like how, outside his office, the people were no longer acting as one would expect them to act.

"Strange fruit!" Jaegwon Choy exclaimed, and dropped whatever it was that had not been a banana directly into his wastebasket, making a beeline for the greenhouse. Within those golden panes of glass, the light was indeed more yellow, and when he entered, he felt as if he had entered not the greenhouse but Biosphere II. For there was no opposite that came to his mind when he saw what the bananas grew from and where the life-sciences students who tended to them had become a part of the emerging Event. Where they had been "evented" through.

And if it was here, it was everywhere, Jaegwon Choy realized with horror. Because, as Alain Badiou had said to him in his younger days, "There is no 'One' and everything that is, is a 'multiple.'"

It was a transition period, with a clear beginning at Biosphere II and an end that was undetermined.

Neighbours of Gordon Nerdrum began to detect signs that something was not quite right with the man. They never saw him. From all sides of his community apartment house, watermarks seeped through to the other tenants' apartment houses—foul-shaped stains that seemed to communicate directly with the tenants' unconscious fears that the sick man had died.

Eventually, all the people who were involved as a result of the watermarks—those below, above, and directly beside Gordon Nerdrum's apartment house, elderly women in cat-eye glasses and cardigan sweaters and their nearly deceased husbands with buzz cuts—met at breakfast over scalding coffee and tea, and together, the big, creased, flabby-eared retirees decided to get the building's general manager to do something about the problem.

The general manager phoned and then knocked. First with his forefinger's knuckle. Then, to the foreknuckle's knock the middle knuckle was added, which made it a bit louder and bonier, before the man knotted his fist and pounded it loudly on the door. When the door continued to block his entrance, the problem left him thinking that these people, whom he often wrote off as senile, were right, and he swallowed his sour saliva and opened the door with a set of clinking master keys.

Pollen blew out into the hallway with the stagnant air from Gordon Nerdrum's apartment house. The space was warm and smelled of mould. There was something balmy and spring-like in the air, a kind of suspicious sweetness. The discoloured walls were damp and ran with water. The air, thick and dense and warm, fogged the general manager's glasses with its enormous breath, so he did not immediately see the dim shape sitting in a chair in the middle of the kitchen.

The creature from Gordon Nerdrum's subconscious had spread. What the general manager couldn't have known was that Gordon Nerdrum, fearing the slime mould, had attempted to burn it alive in the oven. With a crackling, tearing noise, the slime mould had shrivelled up, dried into a black-encrusted blob that smoked and spattered. The general manager saw only the cindery remains and the charred floor. Gordon Nerdrum, having not been able to curb the telepathic words still forming in his head, had tried to save the slime mould, evidenced by the used fire extinguisher, which the general manager nudged with a steeled toe.

Sporification was automatic, and some of the shiny brown spheres had found their way into the dirt of the apartment house's indoor plants. The microscopic spores of the slime mould made many more slime moulds like them, and their multicoloured bodies splattered the walls like a Jackson Pollock.

The general manager, a short, round perspiring man, teetered forward on inferior legs. He knew not that Gordon Nerdrum's hallucinations had been delusional, nor did he know that Gordon Nerdrum's delusional behaviour had been real, and that they were both manifested from his unconscious and his unconscious alone. For the general manager, the facts were missing, but what had emerged from Gordon Nerdrum's head was not.

The kitchen was corrupted by darkness. At its centre sat a nondescript thing that had been Gordon Nerdrum. At that point he heard a voice coming from the organic thing, a voice without words, a groan, as if from underwater, like a song no sirens sing. He was alive, but just what was alive about him was not easy to determine. Fungal forms grew out of a mossy layer that had replaced his epidermis. Other verdant creatures twined down from his contorted fingers and toes in the manner of a root or vine, and around the chair was a circle of large black-gilled mushrooms, which had sprung up out of the mouldering floorboards. At the top of his head, a small sapling had sprouted.

II

Everything trembles, then stops and there is quietness amidst all this fear, like a silent fear seeing another mute fear passing by.

—Fernando Pessoa

One large, unsettling, black car drove through the tall mountains of office buildings and apartment towers, while another circled like a shark in search of prey. These buildings, like miles of greedy stones, added together one by one, like time. An unrelenting time that reigned cement over the collapsing, lifeless kingdom of modern society. A paradise lost to the unutterable sum of banal disappointments. A striving for what one has and what one represents, for the illusion of money and fame. All the while, overcome by the feeling that everything would disappear. Underlying the decay of culture was the fear of accepting both presence and absence. A fear that began as a repulsion, turned to indignation, and then became hatred.

The protests were still going on. The moment the crowd began to disperse, the violence broke out, again. Augustus Lovejoy could make out groups of masked people roaming around with weapons. Windows had been broken, here and there the burned-out husks of cars, buses. The intermittent hoot of a siren, repeatedly wailing, mournful, dim. A blaze in the middle of an intersection.

He grated his teeth and turned pale, but kept unusually calm.

When Augustus Lovejoy arrived, a little late for his meeting, he stopped before the new facade, its many windows merging into one great window, like a sea of reflections with no waves. The shape of the militarized riot police stationed outside, in full Kevlar, stood out clear as a diagram, calmly chatting, with machine guns over their shoulders.

Inside, the din of federal bureaucrats gathered around the bank of elevators like swarms of insects, coming from or going to their respective divisions each day to perform their small tasks, with the sole purpose of accomplishing a series of these tasks; and these tasks, through their repetition, constituted a discrete series of days, the ultimate aim of which, was known only by those who ruled over the glass stories.

●

All the important figures in the city—public, administrative, and commercial—were present.

Augustus Lovejoy knew that what the Institute of Ecotechnics had done through Space Biosphere Ventures was a psychochemical warfare of sorts. And that he and the others, including everyone who had been a part of the third expedition, had acted for the government. Now there was no Institute of Ecotechnics, nor was there even a Space Biosphere Ventures to speak of. Now there was only the serum and the ghosts of those former institutions' involvement in the current administration.

It was after the third expedition when something like an improvised conference between stockholders of the Institute of Ecotechnics and members of the altered-right administration took place. There, Augustus Lovejoy's palm met with many handshakes. When he walked into the dimly lit room, he couldn't immediately make out faces, particularly as the room was filled with a conspiratorial twilight. On one side of the boardroom table, people seemed to be seated with their backs leaning up against the sunset. A man who sat on the windowsill spoke first: "You, Mr. Lovejoy, need to reveal to us all the unknowns."

Augustus Lovejoy raised his gaze to the dark oval throwing out words.

"Don't let's knock heads right off the bat," said a stockbroker fitted into a dull grey suit, his face reflecting experience. "The shareholders of this joint-stock company have gathered here in good faith—faith in Mr. Lovejoy. We are prepared to buy the outline of his enterprise. There's no telling what may happen after. And will somebody flick on a goddamn light?"

The lamplight cast a green glow. The oval face above the windowsill spoke again, the corner of its mouth twitching.

"We need a reasonably inexpensive construction that can hold the thousands of immigrant people and take them to, well..."

"Well, to at least the Mars settlement," growled another voice. "Or can't it take them that far?"

"Don't interrupt, General." The man on the windowsill wanted to go on, but Augustus Lovejoy spoke above them all.

"The ethnic-resettlement program is already well underway. We're past the design phase. Now it's about building more of the same. Within the next few years, we'll begin relocating those presently working in the Canadian labour camps to Mars. They may not like it, but they'll make it there with the impression that it's reparation.

"Now, let's be frank. This isn't what you're hiring me for. You need me to take care of Johannes Van Vyferyken, isn't that right? The competition that has flooded the market because of him has been a constant threat to this enterprise ever since we became a monopoly. Remember: we did not leave him; he left us."

Augustus Lovejoy said this even though he had never really been with them.

There was silence.

"As we all know," he continued, "our country supplies world markets with all sorts of food. This new variety of bacteria is sufficiently robust to withstand compression, dehydration, et cetera so as to reach our consumers all over the world. Immunization shall be kept, of course, strictly for our own use. I needn't describe to you, shareholders and statesmen, what we stand to gain from all of this and the new world we are bound to find.

"In no time, countless bacteria cultures, pressed into cubes, dried and frozen inside all sorts of edibles, sealed into millions of containers, will be on their way to the billions of trusting mouths that will swallow them willingly. Immunization will not go beyond a small circle of top government officials and their retinue. Authorized citizens whose money has gone to building all of this. Namely, all of you."

A man who was accustomed to only answering or not answering posed his first question: "What is to be done about Johannes Van Vyferyken?"

The council shifted in their seats. If the issue had been put to a vote, everyone would have abstained. Augustus Lovejoy's voice alone was enough to ease the tension. The altered-right administration knew it was Johannes Van Vyferyken who was responsible for breaking into the third expedition. And it was a matter of time before they would frame him for what, in truth, the government had done. They would make sure the public saw him as a domestic terrorist, like the Unabomber, a recluse who practiced a nature-centred form of anarchism: dangerous and vengeful. The file would be closed and he would be made to take the blame. Johannes Van Vyferyken would be accountable because somebody always had to be.

Then a watery-eyed engineer with a red face marked by a dull but determined razor tried to smooth the tension over without much success. In boardroom tones, he spoke dryly of costs: "A hundred-person biosphere would increase the cost by fifty percent."

With that, a female stockbroker spoke up, the tissue in her throat hardening: "We've already given the Institute of Ecotechnics everything! Financial support. Political support. Protection from the media. Not to mention my own credibility."

"Please understand," the engineer said obsequiously, "the ethnic-resettlement program will be able to transport refugees to the Mars settlement every two years, when Mars is close to the Earth in its orbit, and it only takes about half that time to actually get there. We will send several shuttles at a time, of course, which should be enough to deal with some of the overflow here on Earth. Then the next action of the program will be to construct the biospheres. Once we know how to inhabit the planet, and adapt the Martian world to our use, you can sell your property and divest."

"Well, all right," the stockbroker said. "But only on one condition: that we have exclusive rights to production and distribution of the serum—here, on Earth, and on the Mars settlement, and anywhere else that a future market may arise, in this system or the next proxy-system. Wherever it will likely be consumed."

"Why?" the general said, in utter suzerainty, his large frame, thick neck, and square face casting a huge shadow in front of the windowsill.

"Very simple: many of our fellow shareholders made a covenant long before an ascetic with a never-ending supply of Phoenix Tears decided to take up preaching in the woods."

"Well, if that's how it is," said another voice. It belonged to a bald man in the corner. Under the shining white glob of his brow, his features huddled in a dead grey triangle. "If that's how it's going to be..."

This remark clashed with another.

Augustus Lovejoy pushed back his chair and stood up. The arguments stopped as he went out into the hall. Beside him bustled one of the clean-shaven stockbrokers, who had a bent back and a briefcase permanently attached to one elbow, like a growth. He was asking questions. They stepped into the narrow elevator together, an elevator that smelled of human sweat ionized on stainless steel. The electric gloom of full-blast panel lighting buzzed and reflected in Augustus Lovejoy's deeply sunken eyes. He supplied no answers. Only at the entrance to the building, his hand in the grip of two damp palms, did Augustus Lovejoy finally say, "I'll get the serum from him. Makes no difference to me if it's you or somebody else who owns it. As long as it's not him."

The palms released his hand.

•

Brown liver spots speckled Augustus Lovejoy's temples. His eyes were bulbous and drooping. Jowls hung underneath them. He had little chin to speak of. His complexion was comparable to that of a drowned person whose body has become slightly discoloured and bloated after several days of drifting downriver and then washes up on the shores of some factory town or the like. His shoulders fallen in, his belly a conspicuous paunch. The blue-grey of his scratchy stubble had the same metallic sheen as the gun holstered in his belt. The gun smelled like his perspective.

His days usually shot by in a blur of meetings. Everything seemed to be rushing at him in that flattened hive of a city and so, as he drove to apprehend Johannes Van Vyferyken for his malpractice and treason—something he would enjoy doing himself, though he could have had somebody else carry out the task—Augustus Lovejoy clenched his fists. He had killed other men, and he would likely kill this man, if he could.

He tried to find some sort of harmony beneath the discord and immersed himself in a long moment of morbid meditation: as his car moved along the tree-lined road, his bald skull—dented in places, glistening with sweat, and crowned with a blistering bump like a horn—swayed methodically.

Usually, he just let impulse drive his actions, but now that the city's mechanical landscape was falling away behind him—for all he knew it was exploding at the point where the lines of the road came together at infinity. And, internally, he repeated the mantra: *Everything is holy. Worship the everyday.*

In his eccentric appropriation of eastern thought, the "now" justified the end. The problem, from his perspective, was less the past than the present. And so, after every night that he slept—or was it with every breath he took?—he awakened reincarnated. *Why not?* He would moult his bad karma, shed the skin and flesh of demon faces for a more divine head, again and again. Shed those hollow forms like a crab sheds its shell, the insect dreams of a past life. Blind and powerless in the shackles of this never-ending dream. Embodiment followed by disembodiment: *Like the stuff in a sausage,* he thought. If it made him feel less guilty, *Why not?* Compassion didn't necessarily prevent cruelty and, in the East, atheism was not a sign of stupidity like it was in the West. Rather, their lack of religion proved their commitment to humanism. Buddhists didn't fear death, or at least what came after death, the afterlife, and neither did he.

He recalled Mao Zedong's old motto: "Everything under heaven is in utter chaos; the situation is excellent." Indeed, everything was excellent, if not for himself alone. Which is what he figured Mao meant when he said this to the thousands of Chinese who had lost members of their family to the tyranny of the People's Republic of China. *They were afraid of the face of God*, Augustus Lovejoy thought. *Everyone fears seeing what God is, and Mao had the face of God. Therefore, the people of China feared him.* Like Mao, Augustus Lovejoy was running his own revolution: the USENA.

When the United Nations dissolved, a new international body was formed: the USENA—the United States of Europe and America. This was largely in response to the East's rising up as a new economic power through superintelligent AI.

The smarter-than-human, decision-making AI systems of both China and Russia had arrived at unexpected and extreme solutions that had aggressively cut out the West from trade with an embargo, dealing a lethal blow to the USENA. Germany, with its strategic culture—pessimistic about China and optimistic about Russia—was the only Western country that could continue to afford trade with the East and for whom the Eastern government's sanction had been negotiated to make an exception.

Immigration hadn't stopped in Europe, as it had in America, even after the Slovakian countries rolled out barbed tape so as to prevent refugees from entering. The wealthier, more liberal Eurocentric countries of the USENA, detached from the issue as they were, established a kind of Allies-versus-Axis relationship with these non-Western European countries. The Eurocentric countries hypocritically criticized the Slovakian countries for their anti-immigration position while accusing them of letting through the immigrants who did make it into the black heart of Europe. Those who made it through, of course, went straight for those most invested in democracy.

Those countries, with their larger, noisier, and more chaotic cities, went straight for Augustus Lovejoy. They needed a "transition to peaceful development," and he had promised those influencers of society that he could create human machinery capable of servicing their society, the utility of this human machine being precisely that it delivered total control. His automatons, his society, his final empire was what he had promised those countries.

"An ethical machine, built according to the latest advances in morals and technology," he had told nationalists all over the world. "An experiment to create an artificial observer. An artificial hell. A machine that takes control of only those human movements and muscular contractions that have a clear social significance. Because a handful of soldiers is always better than a mouthful of arguments."

Even in the Canadian interior, from Alberta through Saskatchewan and into Manitoba, labour camps toiled. There were no longer any penitentiaries or executions, but there was the penalty of endless work. The proof that they lived was that sometimes they died. And many died before their service was up, and it was easy to end up there. The only place left for the USENA to obtain the raw materials they needed to compete with the Eastern nations was in those dreary labour camps. The embargo and its butterfly effect touched everything.

Now, limited in resources, the USENA had to either reduce the population or leave Earth. It was likely that they were going to have to do both, and it was looking like the serum was going to do this for them. But in that same place where Augustus Lovejoy drew his strength, where every revolutionary drew their revolutionary opinions from, was a secret conviction that nothing could be changed. A superstitious token that he used when trying to change things, only to prevent the change from ever actually happening.

•

In the distance, Augustus Lovejoy could see first one then many pillars of smoke spreading across the coastline, like serpents on their way to meet him. He was too late; Johannes Van Vyferyken had anticipated their coming and had set aflame all the property that they would have seized: the biofabricated house, the chapel, and the lab beneath it. They were all beyond rescue by the time he and his team had reached the acreage: charred shells, hissing and steaming.

Only the redwoods remained under a sepia sun and a grey sky that looked as if it had been rubbed with a soiled eraser. The redwoods stood apprehensively and in rebellion against the hungry flames that had consumed the undergrowth, somehow striking out against Augustus Lovejoy. Like a portal, the solid door of the chapel remained upright in its frame; the rest of the building had been reduced to cinder and ash.

Augustus Lovejoy cursed aloud as his operatives pulled over their vehicles and joined him on the side of the metalled road. He had left things too much to chance, and now his luck had abandoned him. They watched the scapegoat burn. *What now?*

In the sky, above even the enormous redwoods, a bird circled the great billowing columns of sparks and black fumes. The bird was large, like a falcon—he couldn't guess the species. It was like nothing he had ever seen or would ever see again.

If it's Johannes Van Vyferyken, thought Augustus Lovejoy, *then it's because that bastard finally decided to practice what he preaches.*

Of course, there was no way of knowing.

One of the operatives—a would-be lumberjack who stood near the vehicles in a bright multicoloured plaid shirt with sleeves rolled up to the elbows and jeans and boots that looked too new to be worn by a Canadian—must have been thinking the same thing, as he tried to aim his gun at the bird. The gun used for hunting people had suddenly become a gun for hunting fowl. But before the man could shoot, Augustus Lovejoy gestured for him to lower the firearm. There was no sense killing what was already dead, or at least no longer alive in the same way.

But as is the way with all things too good to be true, a moment later, the bird's gliding, scaly light joined with smell and sound as it coursed down to join the inferno. Neither hide nor hair remained.

In the moment of change, Augustus Lovejoy closed his mind to talk. Feeling disturbed and thinking hard, he heard a sentence start pronouncing itself in his unconscious mind, each word equally weighted: I killed Johannes Van Vyferyken.

It was a lie. He was used to telling untruths but not to himself. It was what he had wanted to be able to say, that he killed Johannes Van Vyferyken. But he would never say it because whether or not Johannes Van Vyferyken was dead was unimportant. He had not killed him. The one most responsible among all those responsible had escaped.

Around his vision edged a blackness. His eyes became ineffective and useless to him. Hatred had turned them to obsidian. Hatred and a desire for hatred. What connected his body to the planet, his body-planet interface, was temporarily severed, and he was soon squatting then sitting on the ground, looking like a garden Buddha who had nodded off.

He struggled against a vision: In the dark, he was walking on a footpath through mountains in Tibet. The path was wide enough for only one traveller. Eventually, he came upon that dreaded other traveller heading in the opposite direction. It was Johannes Van Vyferyken, though in the body of a Tibetan, adorned with clothing and mannerisms that suggested noble status, his bearded face muffled up to the eyes in the folds of his flowing cloak. Neither moved. And then, Augustus Lovejoy, in the body of a less-important

Tibetan, wrapped in ragged, many-coloured stuffs, his stubbornly boney brow bowed, unpursed his thin, shrivelled lips for the sake of a single, brief-as-a-blow "no." Made an idiotic face, as if to demonstrate his utter stupidity, and jumped from the path on the mountainside into the abyss. He was inferior, and this action was proof of that.

Cruelty towards another was of an altogether different order from cruelty upon oneself. There was a dark stupidity in Augustus Lovejoy's bestial impulse to inflict suffering on others. He had not turned his spirit into a living sacrifice and felt a bitter sort of admiration for his old enemy, who had so thoroughly stripped himself of all life in the search for knowledge.

He returned to real-time, with vertigo still present. There followed an interval of several minutes, moments when the vision took over again. The brief illusion of another existence. A parallel version of himself. He was boiling with anger and had no clear objective. The operatives were hesitantly helping him up. He shrugged them off, stretched his legs, and then he recalled something. A woman driving in the other direction on the highway below. Maybe an hour back. He realized now that he recognized her. She was an odd woman. A scientist. Her work was in active protest of the serum. Presumably, she had been here to find out more about the drug's origin and indirectly found out who the operatives were. It was possible that she even had a concentrated version of the serum, which would be worse for the government than losing their original scapegoat. She had become complicitous without knowing it. That's how it worked. Getting involved. Becoming a person of interest. The suspicion would get on you without your knowing where it was, as if it were a tiny bug beetling just under the threshold of detection.

It was a mistake to come here, he thought and stepped on a mushroom murderously. His failure had surprised him. He was pierced to the core by it. And that momentary error filled him with outrage. It was a complete mistake, and the error, the homicidal outrage, in turn, filled the whole universe with his unwavering fury. Another universe emerged. Grim, joyless, and mean. His sight, nourished by grinding hatred, disgust, and fear, exploded into paranoia, and eventually, his gaze was deranged, portending where these sentiments would find more bloodthirsty excuses. There was still not enough violent satisfaction. Still not enough exultant revenge. There never would be.

He stopped, choking with indignation, and went over to the operatives.

"Are you going to fucking let her get away or what?!" There's no doubt, none at all: they had no choice. He smiled with disdain, already thinking more about the woman than about Johannes Van Vyferyken. He was still going to release his cruelty, and enjoy every second.

For Augustus Lovejoy, Johannes Van Vyferyken was like the pebble that had put a dent in his windshield on the ride up and the woman the crack that had spidered out since. He would have to take care of it before the problem spread in all directions.

2035, Summer

He had been kicked within the biosphere. Kicked violently within the biosphere by news from the outside.

Sunlight coming in through the enclosure's glass ceiling always had a different look about it. It wasn't enough light for some of the lower-lying plants to photosynthesize, and it made everything outside seem glassier than it was. Glass clouds. Glass sky. Glass landscape. Everything outside was glass because he himself was in the glass enclosure. And when he saw his reflection, it was like trying to reconcile two stereoscopic images so that a third would emerge. It never did.

The rows of Arizona mountains were like corroded teeth. Rusty and red. A caravan of migrants passed through, and as Johannes Van Vyferyken watched their curious formation through the biosphere's windows, he could feel the weight of empty time hanging over the migrants. They seemed translucent, as if the desert landscape showed through their bodies, as if they had been experienced but not yet recognized by him. Not yet recognized by anyone.

Human beings did better as nomads, Johannes Van Vyferyken thought. *All our problems came about after we stopped moving. Because shelter is illusory. Because we never should have stopped wandering. We were designed not to stay in one spot for too long. To stop moving is death for us.*

He watched the lines of a woman's contours, sometimes running suggestively thick and sometimes suggestively thin. She lay naked in the nearest sleeping pod. The chamber of sleeping pods was small but big enough to make the double-backed beast. This would be the last time. For, like most of the biospherians, Ekaterina Korytko had a life on the outside and had chosen child-rearing over pair-bonding, whereas Johannes Van Vyferyken had not.

The two years was over, and they would be released later that day. There was already talk of a third mission. New investors. Ideological traffic. People in the pharmacology industry who wanted to fund the ideology and so own it. Own an imaginary relationship to a real situation. A simulation. Because that's what an ideology was: a nonentity.

"We're supposed to be post-ideological—why do we keep falling for the same mistakes?" he asked unemotionally, turning from the window and moving to the long, prostrate body. Ekaterina Korytko's head was now propped up by her arm at a right angle in an expression of interest. "Because, in reality, we are inside this hermetically sealed vessel, living our lives as if it is our own hermetically sealed state system, way of life, culture... acting as if the problems of the hermetically sealed are all solved. And they're not. They're just not..."

He followed the endless curves of her body with his hand, caressed the cherry-coloured pressure bruising she had gotten from both the farm work in the agricultural biome and the air pressure in the dome. The bruises were the same purply colour as her nipples,

nipples that blossomed like nocturnal flowers at the centre of each breast, breasts like silvery drops of water dripping over either side of her chest. On her thigh was a tattoo of an *ensō*: a circle drawn with an opening.

Their love was orgasmic love, and they had loved ecstatically since that first orgasm. They had seized this chance at immortality, their chromosomes humming loudly in all the startling attraction and sexual dimorphism that made sex good. At first, he'd had a hard time maintaining an erection because of the antipsychotics he was on, which presented challenges, but this turned out, in the end, to be more of a psychological impotence than a physiological one. Her excitement, their passion, allowed his erection to spring freely, free of worry.

Before his sex-love with Ekaterina Korytko, Johannes Van Vyferyken had shown little emotion to any of the biospherians. All the heavy stresses and emotional shocks that came with managing the biosphere for five years had triggered the return of a past trauma: the time that he had spent in hospital isolation as a child. An epidermal infection with a fever like a religious euphoria. Rashes that left their scars on his adult body. He had never been the same toward others after that, and the social calculus required of him to manage the biosphere project was often almost obviously too much. He had always felt physical pain whenever he came into contact with human beings, as if he had been somehow disqualified from being a human being. But she had been his second chance at something better, something besides endless work. He had escaped from his dread of human beings into her arms, into the slow rise and fall of her white breasts, the childlike sleep which dissipated his fear. He felt absolutely secure sleeping soundly in a night of repose with this kindred woman: Ekaterina Korytko. He felt a kind of happiness and liberation. And now this too had passed.

Because everything passes.

As dawn came and went through the biosphere's transparent walls, the tastelessness of nature attested itself in distant purples, colours briefly seen through a grubby white that seemed to conceal a pale, almost-imagined yellow.

The fear of losing her had defeated his rebellion. Not knowing how it would all end up, the full horror of the possibility of such love became all the more realistic. He ached and dripped with a sad uncompromising romantic seriousness, knowing, as he did, that this rather adolescent conflict of passions would never quite go away. He had never been so close to happiness. It had marked him forever.

The kindred woman spoke to him now as though he were a patient, clinically pausing between her word-perfect descriptions: "Fear. Anxiety. Depression. Shame. Guilt. Avoidance of intimacy. These are all the consequences that can be tied to difficulties in our relationships, in our self-image, our mind-body connection, as they used to say." Ekaterina Korytko knew there was a strong placebo effect when it came to ED caused by severe forms of stress; she led counselling groups on the outside and dealt with the derealization that struck down most of the biospherians. "But you can be helped. Belief can help you. The strength of belief in your new life." She slapped the flat of her hand on his flank, hard and grabby, and turned abruptly away, as if to say, "Going to put some clothes on?" and then did so herself, stepping into her biosuit before reentering the other biomes in preparation for depressurization.

The scarlet smear of her handprint was still fading from his numb and swollen cheek. He stood there in a kind of dumb sentience, his limp penis hanging like a flag with no wind. *When habit ends, then what? Is that when real change occurs?*

The moment Johannes Van Vyferyken walked out of Biosphere II, he would have to surrender the future of the project to Augustus Lovejoy. A forced paradigm of unnoticed consent would descend upon him from above. Symptomatically, he felt the strengthening in his receptive mode and the weakening in his mode of action. Those habitual psychological structures that organize, limit, select, and interpret perceptual incentives were being taken away. It was a hard truth to accept, one which he didn't think he would ever accept, not really.

•

The biomes were geologically and environmentally stable by the end of the second year, which occurred during the second phase. Space might be an impossible adaptation, but if what they had done here was done in a crater on the Moon, it might just work. Russia had already been running simulations for years in Arctic towns, and they would probably be up there soon. First industrializing the Moon, then terraforming Venus and Mars and select asteroids along the way. The Moon was the gateway to space; it was a research station, and everything else depended on how the Moon base went.

Johannes Van Vyferyken didn't often leave his lichen farm in the bacteriological lab, but when he did, it was usually to help the others with the harvest or to ease tensions between the resident crew. It was a pocket of post-scarcity that dissolved at the borders, a blue dome on the Arizona horizon's Martian-like terrain. Sometimes he thought they were already on the Mars settlement. Borderless and free.

This was his second go at managing the direction of the project, and it was not without a considerable power struggle that he had maintained the position for as long as he had. The first time, they'd had to exit early because oxygen levels had dropped too low and die-offs of many animal and plant species—a result of species packing—had occurred in greater numbers than anticipated. Near the end, the hungry biospherians, refusing to come out of their biosphere early, were eating seed stock that hadn't yet been grown.

This time, they had achieved total food sufficiency and hadn't needed any oxygen injections. And that was why they were being taken over. Not because they had failed the first time, but because they had learned to fail better the second.

Johannes Van Vyferyken made his routine run through the west lung's vertical farming operation. The LED lamps configured to specific wavelengths made him blink. The biome ran with zero effect: no runoff, no pests or parasites, no external weather conditions. The vertical stacks of food and medicine were produced without a threat.

He continued through to the lunar greenhouse and its bioregenerative life-support system, which would hopefully grow vegetables on the Moon by recycling and purifying water through plant transpiration. Since the Moon wouldn't have a proper hydrological cycle until it was bombarded by ice asteroids, transpiration would have to do.

After the lunar greenhouse, he visited Landscape Evolution Observation. He could already smell something organic in the air: it was the smell of earth, soil, where all life started and seemed to remain even in the worst ecological catastrophes. What had been millions of pounds of nonliving, abiotic volcanic rock was slowly developing over several years into a rich soil capable of supporting microbial and vascular plant life. He even used it for his own biologically robust bacteria colonies.

All the scientists of the cooperative had, hamstrung though they were by research contracts with big corporations, collaborated in some capacity with the project at large to prove that the Anthropocene was unequivocally linked to humanity's impact on the planet. Small demonstrations of a much bigger picture. A picture that one day life would spread through the universe and that humans would be responsible for who, what, when, where, why, and how it spread. It was what science had always seemed to work toward, from horror vacui to life on other planets. The scientist as hero, as shepherd god, would become interplanetary and so steward the Earth out of the fear of extinction. Or at least that was the goal. The only teleological goal that mattered enough to become a norm.

Being in the biome was almost a religious experience for Johannes Van Vyferyken now, a mystical psychosis, like the fever of his youth, though it had been only a venture into the realm of viriditas: the greening power, the green surge, the pulse of life. The air, like the sunlight, was also different from the air he would breathe on the outside, and for him, that made it a different world. He was full of it and it was full of him. In a way, they had left the planet and returned as outsiders—somehow younger and somewhat wiser than before. Biospherians. That's what the media had been calling them.

After making his final rounds, Johannes Van Vyferyken returned to the lichen farm of his bacteriological lab. The arrays of eukaryote strains that contained his plasmid would likely have their place as keystones in the logic of future coexistence. The weird substance was soon to be controlled through patent as an Easy Think Substance for Easy Think Ethics. He only had to adjust the focus of his electronic microscope slightly for the eukaryotic cells, which to the unaided eye looked like a small and spongy lacework of organic matter, to take on the generously enlarged qualities of stained glass. A more functional analogy would be to compare the plasmid to a machine. A soft machine with purifiable cells that could be incorporated into other cells. An ecology without nature. A kind of Fordist notion, complete with exchangeable parts.

There was a burst of light right in his eye. The microscope created a hallucinatory vision for him, a visual meditation that dispensed with his thinking of words until he accidently began to think. *And thinking is no longer meditation*, he thought. *Thinking leads to objectivity.* But he was wrong in his visual meditation. As a visual witness, he was the victim of error, a purely optical error, he was defective in various ways, though error was the inevitable way in which he worked. He knew this and so, no longer meditating, soon succumbed to the danger of "logic" instead of "seeing."

The plasmid DNA was a circle that could be open or closed. In the former case, the circle was incomplete, allowing for movement and development as well as the perfection of all things. The beauty of imperfection was free to be expressed. Wabi-sabi. When the circle was closed, it represented perfection. Plato's perfect form.

This work was a spiritual practice for Johannes Van Vyferyken, a ritual, and he continued without respite. To him it meant enlightenment, strength, elegance, the universe, and the void. Uninhibited moments when his mind was free to let these bodies create gene expressions with both the character of their creator and the context of their creation; the creation being both a natural and human-made object. And once he gave expression to them, he didn't change them. They changed themselves in one continuous period of time. The plasmid had its own ritual within its cells—a mark of life—and every cell was born with the same ritual, and every cell experienced the same destiny of the ritual. But in each double-stranded molecule, he'd had to program that period of time to end in cell death. Mandatory suicide genes in all GMO trials were regulation. And so he'd come to acknowledge three simple realities: nothing lasts, nothing is finished, and nothing is perfect.

It was shocking to say, but Johannes Van Vyferyken had to admit, his eukaryotes had just as much a right to exist as human beings, a nonhuman right. But that sort of kindness was never perfectly automated in human beings. One simply couldn't extend rights to all nonhuman things all at once—it would be nonsense to do so.

The thoughtform viriditas manifests in human consciousness as ecognosis, Johannes Van Vyferyken thought, as he watched the cells, lean and withered, become emptiness. *Approximately 90 percent of the cells in the human body belong to nonhuman organisms; bacteria, fungi, and a whole bestiary of other organisms. Why shouldn't this also be the case for human thought as well?*

Ecognosis was a gigantic thought. A double-thought, a double-idea. It wasn't just thinking ecologically or socially but the structure of thought as nonhuman. *An ecological politics that you would have to be intoxicated into realizing. Humans without nature are humans without pattern are humans without thought are humans without humans.*

And although he didn't know it was seeing him, he didn't know that a plasmid saw, they were looking at each other. But if its eyes were not seeing him, its existence was experiencing him. In the world Johannes Van Vyferyken was coming to know, a world of viriditas, of ecognosis, there were several ways of *seeing*: a looking at the other without seeing; a possessing the other; an eating the other; a being in a place; and a being in a place with the other being there, too. The plasmid wasn't seeing him directly; it was with him. The plasmid wasn't seeing him with its eyes but with its body. And Johannes Van Vyferyken—he was seeing. There was no way not to see.

The whole operation was about to become a technology under the new management, a fully automated AI computer to control the systems of Biosphere II and interact with the biospherian crew. *The fewer the managers, the greater the manageability.* He was sure it would be made into a weapon, the way all science and technology in America was made into a weapon. But those taking over would have to wait until the Moon was properly industrialized for that; it was too high risk an experiment to carry out on Earth. Because, in reality, simulating a bioplague was equivalent to creating one. Equivalent to creating a biological heresy.

If those venture capitalists taking charge of the project did go through with the bioplague experiment, there would be no end to their troubles in the global capitalist paradise. And when regressive conditions forced transnationals to multinationalize, and multinationals to nationalize, maybe then they would become ecologically aware of themselves as a species. Maybe then they would stop with their denial of the species. *A human species with many horizontal cousins and not just food grown in vats*, Johannes Van Vyferyken thought with a sense of serene melancholy and perhaps also a spiritual longing, as he finished sterilizing his lab of any and all remnants of its former viriditas, its former, clinging life.

On her cell phone, Céline Høltermand drove as she listened to her colleague explain how their lab had been raided the night before. "Raided like we were a clinic, like we didn't have temporary permits to research the stuff. I showed them the official papers. They didn't care."

She listened to the shaking voice of her colleague with disgust and despair. It was too late for her colleagues; they were already giving up, with fear and shattering.

"Where are you phoning me from?" Céline Høltermand asked.

"They took us in for questioning. I was just released from an interrogation. Don't go back to the lab. There isn't anything left. They took everything." Her colleague's voice lowered, became the bass in the conversation's score. "I mean, I don't think you can even cross the border right now."

"What do you mean?" She couldn't control her voice, and it trilled and quavered like a bird with clipped wings.

"The government declared a state of emergency. I think there are a lot of bad batches of the stuff going around. They're trying to contain it. Don't go back if you don't have to. It's too late. Also, they were asking about you."

"Who was asking about what?"

"I don't know exactly."

"What did they say?"

"They were saying that your work, our work, our involvement with the drug in the context of the present crisis, puts us under suspicion of domestic terrorism." Her colleague paused. "Those were the words they used: *domestic terrorism.*"

"Thanks for phoning. I'll touch base with you if I run into trouble at the border. Take care of yourself." Céline Høltermand hung up, feeling as if someone else had begun listening to their call the moment the term *domestic terrorism* came up.

Of course, she couldn't cross the border now that she had the drug. What was she going to do with it? She couldn't be caught in possession of it, so how was she going to study it? Study it with what equipment and where? She had to either dispose of it or ingest it.

Paranoia wedged its way between the head and heart of Céline Høltermand and left her ajar as it dug deeper inside that nameless place, inside the tombs of the unconscious. Earlier, a motorcade had hurtled past her like a demonic force with unknown human intent. Now, hours later, in the rearview mirror, then the side mirrors, she eyed the same vehicles behind her. Was it the paranoia or were the half a dozen black sedans and SUVs with tinted windows following her? She wondered if they'd started following her after she left Johannes Van Vyferyken's acreage or commune or whatever it was. *What would cause them to do that?*

She didn't actually know much about Canada. She had never really visited the country. Never left the United States of America. As far as she knew, the Canadian cities were full of spies, full of blurry, fuzzy espionage. As Canada was a neutral nation, both information and money were transferred here and became politically charged elsewhere. She might be able to negotiate with someone once she reached Vancouver, but how would she know that it wouldn't lead her into something even more incriminating?

She thought the motorcade might pass if she slowed down, but instead it also slowed. So, she accelerated; her vehicle tore at the pavement and that seemed to work—the motorcade didn't speed up. But the main road was the only road; they had to know that she wasn't making much of a difference for herself by gaining a mile or two.

Céline Høltermand balled her fists on the wheel until her knuckles turned white. Free of worry was the inverse of what she felt. She felt the stammering uncertainty of desperation. She was fighting something that was changing all the time. She didn't know where her efforts were taking her. All she knew for sure was that she was driving from northern British Columbia to Vancouver and that there may or may not be people following her. And if there were, they would soon find out that she was taking them nowhere.

She was trying to steer, or rather she pretended to steer, but basically, she didn't understand anything anymore. She saw she was low on gas—about a quarter tank was left. Soon she would be entirely out of gas. The highway was strangely empty. She hadn't passed a single car in over a hundred kilometers, and she started to think she was going crazy. She turned on the car radio, but it didn't work. Full of static, crackling. Something was happening.

As Céline Høltermand approached Vancouver, with only an hour or so till she reached the city, she started to see vehicles parked off to the side of the highway. The number of vehicles made her half expect a search party to be combing the woods, forming a long chain of humans linked to humans. She realized this was the break she needed and jumped at the opportunity to be the missing person they found, so that she wouldn't have to confront alone those she suspected of following her.

She had put some distance between her and them over the last hour and could take advantage of the interval of time. They were using what discretion they had. She pulled the car over, and it skidded on the loose gravel before coming to a complete stop. She grabbed her camera from the passenger seat and the serum and dispenser from the glove box. Céline Høltermand loaded the dispenser, considered taking it, considered not taking it, and then headed into the forest.

The shore wasn't far from the road; she could hear waves slapping against waves. Not finding any signs of a trail, she passed under the trees and moved into the yawning forest on a root-buckled path. Unlike the redwood forest, this one wasn't dominated by any one tree in particular. But like the redwood forest, there was something uncanny about it. At random, she came upon a birch tree. And then another. She expected that at some point on her way to the shore the forest would transition into nothing but birch trees. It did not.

She called out several times, each time louder. No one answered.

Then a thought struck her still. *Men kill men differently than they do women.* She imagined what the men of the motorcade would do to her. Her camera rose and fell like a pendant as her chest heaved. The tension that had built up inside her was moving out and into the trees. It was as if her anxiety were integrating into the ecology around her; into the trees whose dark spots were like the eyes of something soft and wounded wrapped in a series of transparent veils.

The grove of birch trees made her think of the Celtic belief that the souls of those who have been lost are held captive in some inferior being—in an animal, in a plant, in some inanimate object— and so are effectively lost.

She wore the camera eye before her face like an ornate Venetian mask with a single cyclopean eye; the camera's shutter opened and closed, capturing the grim and imposing majesty of the peculiar groupings of birch. She was unsurprised when they turned out the same as the ghost pictures she'd taken at Johannes Van Vyferyken's acreage: overexposed. But when she stopped streaming through the reel to zoom in on one of the photographs, she noticed a kind of double-image. Almost as if she had performed a double-exposure on the birch trees. The trees appeared translucent, almost like semi-reflective glass, letting some light in but refracting the rest away, which would account for the overexposed image. Ghosting through the birches' hologram were what seemed to resemble pixelated pseudo-human figures, motionlessly telling their story, their history, in a frozen mirror-realm, a silvery tableau.

At this, she dropped the camera, and it smashed hard against the living granite beneath her feet, narcissistic stones only half-covered by nature's carpet. Was this what had become of the people who owned those deserted vehicles? If so, she didn't know what names to engrave into their bark; she couldn't release them if they had turned into these trees. Who would say her name to break this spell if she herself became bound by it? Did it even need to be broken? Would she, too, be trapped as a birch or some other arbitrary thing among things? Blinking back tears that ran down her neck, she tried to pressure herself into taking the serum, but that didn't work, and so, in resignation, she slumped back against one of the birch trees.

Maybe, after taking the drug, I'll change over into a sea slug. The sea slug cannot suffer. It has no central nervous system, no centre of experience, she told herself. *There is no there-there. But what would that existence be like? It is equally not described by its opposite—that is, a being capable of suffering intelligently. Should we say the sea slug is dead or alive? What can we say of that which is neither?*

She started walking and found no one when the forest cleared onto a rocky beach with round and smooth wood turned by the sea. There was a heavily wooded island, just beyond swimming distance, whose pine forest looked like the spiked back of some monstrous beast that only came up for air every thousand years. She could see the curve of the land from which she had come. It had seemed straighter while she was driving. The atmosphere seemed filled with creeping movements. A smoky scent suggested there was a forest fire within driving distance of the area; the haze made a red disk of the sun above her.

Céline Høltermand also smelled rot in the air, and the buzzing of insects nearby alerted her to a gelatinous mass of rotting blubber at the edge of the beach. A whale, or at least she thought it was a whale. Capsized. Upside down so that the grooves and lines that made tracks along its stomach faced the sky. Stranded on shore, it had either collapsed under its own weight, or died of dehydration, or, judging by the position of its submerged blowhole, drowned at high tide, for the dead hulk still heaved and gurgled, involuntarily, in the foaming waves.

She decided then that she would take the drug. If only to become beached, as this whale had. Like the whale, she had come too close to something that she did not have the biological equipment to escape. Or maybe she had it all wrong and the whale had been someone like her, someone trying to escape with the biological equipment they did have but could not control.

Freedom is a secret, she thought, with a tranquil, neutral ferociousness. *A continuous freedom to exit* my *world and enter* the *world.*

A car alarm went off back in the direction of the highway. There was no clap of thunder that would have set it off on its own. The men would be sure to search it and then, finding nothing, come the way she had.

Violence never seemed real until now.

Maybe I have chosen to die, she thought, not knowing where to turn. *No: I'm incapable of choosing to die. There's just no other way.* She was going to take the drug. If she did, they wouldn't be able to kill her. They'd have failed. She was going to take it. This was it. She'd like it to be over. They'd keep coming if she didn't. And once they had seen her, she'd start yelling. No, she'd be screaming. She'd still be completely conscious and they'd be sure to leave her completely conscious.

Panicked flight. Sweating all over. She'd been suddenly stricken with cosmic fear.

The mysterious fidelity that she had for herself had pushed her towards this risk, towards this death. Now, she was at the centre of fear. From this centre she went towards the vanished image of her life. Here she fought an invisible battle. The blood in her body flowed loudly. Her heart was beating too fast. Death was inside her. The veins in her arm ached with it. Over her pulse, there was a painful throbbing on the wrist. She needed to stop the throbbing, stop the heart from pounding. But it wouldn't calm down on its own; it needed help. *When this heart stops beating,* she thought, *it will all be over.*

The dispenser was loaded with the serum from the episode of earlier indecision. Céline Høltermand steeled herself. Mastered her breath. Becoming strangely self-possessed. She put a dazzling spot of the oil on the pad of her finger and then licked it off herself like a house cat licks its paws. She looked into the water that edged onto the land as her reflection faded from it. It was only the reflection of a mask hiding this true self. The aura of the woman she had once been, through and forgotten.

There was something new. It happened in an instant. Where was she? What's happening to her? No more pounding. It wasn't that anymore. She felt her face change, change. She was scared. Shivers at the back of her neck. She was changing, changing. Her heart stopped its pounding. She had changed. She was afraid. She didn't feel her heart anymore. It was over. Because now there was something new.

Strength shifted under her skin. As her body metabolized the concentrate, her skin sprouted fur and she fell to all fours like a great beast from a dream, rippling orange-black.

2040, Autumn

"One day I will shed my skin like a phoenix in a fire to become some new creature of the deepest sun. From God to ash and dust to human! We are becoming, and becoming is the all-encompassing unity of reality."

Johannes Van Vyferyken's voice boomed in the darkness, and there was no echo in the sunless room because the chapel was too small for such an impressive sound. The acoustic particles of his voice, the eternal chord of beautiful and distorted sounds that resonated from it, made beautiful and distorted patterns that were visible, geometrically archetypal designs that emerged from the nervous systems of those in the congregation, with their altered states of consciousness.

"But for now, I am here and this is me. Where spiritual and physical health are one, I am who I am. Where the divine world and the divine nature are one, I am who I will be. Assume your true form and we will be one on the inside, uniform, as one, forever."

At this juncture, the entire congregation was summoned to chant the many meanings of viriditas: "Virility. Freshness. Greening. Life. Vitality. Fertility. Fecundity. Fruitfulness. Verdure. Growth. Homeostasis."

Everything had to have a pattern, and at this revelation some smiled—smiled at the almost insane sensitivity to order they felt had been achieved by Johannes Van Vyferyken's litany of words and, overcome by a happy sense of satisfaction, danced in a frenzy of activity. Others simply closed their eyes angrily, disbelieving the disturbing voices and feeling terribly serious about whatever arrangement the geometrical forms affecting various parts of their visual systems might take next. In an inverted celebration, the congregation began to speak in tongues of fire and, as during the month-long dark retreats some had taken in the caves and underground corridors on the acreage, many saw light without light actually entering their eyes. A liturgy of light.

Johannes Van Vyferyken's inflamed skin cells began to burn and sting. Raised, itchy red bumps appeared in patches that moved around the surface of his body. Pinpoint-sized dots spreading to welts inches in diameter. These evanescent wheals, skin lesions, lingered anywhere from twenty-four hours to six weeks. Chronic hives of unknown cause: stress, probably. If he knew the trigger, he could have simply avoided it, but it could have been anything: medication, food, food poisoning, autoimmune reaction, allergic or nonallergic reaction, viral or bacterial infection, cold exposure, sun exposure, water contamination, or even exercise or sustained pressure on the skin. The swelling did not become visible quickly; his hands, feet, trunk, abdomen, buttocks, legs, and face all betrayed the appearance of normal hands, feet, trunk, abdomen, buttocks, legs, and face. But neither the hives nor his behaviour was normal, with or without a discernible trigger.

During the sermon, as an act of communion, Johannes Van Vyferyken put a single wafer on the outstretched, soon-to-be-cloven tongues of each of his followers. "Eat life and be eaten by life," he said in a vampiric fashion. "I am no occultist. I don't believe that everything ends in everything; for me, everything begins in everything. Our kingdom is this world. And only through the Hell inside of us can we see what Hell is like. Because Hell is a world fully alive."

An ergot-like parasitic fungus had been used to consecrate the flour with which the wafer was made. A variant of the G2-type common fungus found in grasses from moist forest and mountain habitats. It contained lysergic acid and the plasmid. The plasmid that moved its evolutionary patterns through all the eukaryotic life on the acreage, to widen outwards and into the surround, the swirling shell of viriditas, the deep interior of life.

The environment itself had become a gigantic object; not simply a background but a mesh: a spiralling network of interconnection without centre or edge. A Ganzfeld environment rendering here and there, up and down, foreground and background meaningless. A happy nihilism.

There are two types of ergotism, and both result in poisoning. The first type, which Johannes Van Vyferyken served up as the ancient Greeks had, as a drink called kykeon, was characterized by muscle spasms, fever, and hallucinations. Appearing dazed, unable to speak, becoming manic, his followers would sometimes have all these reactions and more—forms of paralysis or tremors and other distorted perceptions—until recovery or else death occurred. All happening within minutes after consumption.

The second type, which was in the wafer, was marked by a violent burning in the limbs and a pulsing, shooting pain in the fingers and toes. The phoenix spread its wings out through the fingertips of the congregation. When Johannes Van Vyferyken could hear "the voice of heaven" or see "the shade of the living light," all that he was doing was illuminated. When he had no visions of unification, the sadness and joy gave way to the horror and sorrow of what he had done.

Johannes Van Vyferyken started to experience visions himself, as if he had taken a lasting dose of bad acid, although he hadn't ingested the wafers or the kykeon. The visions could have been due to working with the hallucinogenic component present in the ergot-like organism—the substance-producing kernels with the active ingredients extracted for the serum concentrate—or to some kind of scintillating scotoma. But if it was the latter, the migraine produced no pain.

It was, however, what one did with a psychological condition that was important, not the invalidation that it was caused by this or that or the other thing. And what Johannes Van Vyferyken had done through his progressively worsening psychological condition was produce a pharmakon: a remedy followed by a poison followed by a scapegoat. Pharmacology and toxicology were nothing without the pharmakos ritual of human sacrifice. The pharmakon didn't always work. It was imperfect. And so this third sense of the word with its three meanings had never been more obscure to Johannes Van Vyferyken than when those inner visions of the shade of the living light stopped. For when this happened and the morning sun resounded over that dark splendour, he found himself in a room full of half-dead bodies, made miserable because their limbs had fallen off.

The Cult of the Phoenix had kept working, totally resigned to their fate: sowing the crops and tilling the vegetable plantations and harvesting the useful wheat to extract the drug hidden amid gigantic fields spreading to the horizon. They had poisoned the crops and the ground and the people using them. A zombie substance for zombie humans. A walking death.

With the placid face of a doctor, Johannes Van Vyferyken placed them, one by one, in burial suits infused with mushroom mycelia. Mycelia which had been trained with hair and skin flakes and tweezers and Petri dishes to enjoy eating human flesh. Then, plot by plot, he put them in flat-packed, slotted cardboard coffins. A funeral for his future children, singing from the grave. The mushrooms would digest them in two days. Metabolizing even the mercury in their bodies as they did so. Decomponauts. It gave their death meaning: death fed life.

•

Everything came to an end that day. A supernatural light had followed the rain, and when the sun left the valley to set behind the mountains, all of his worshippers lost consciousness.

That day Johannes Van Vyferyken had spent part of the afternoon in the shed near the marshes mangrove forest where he kept the game he hunted. Four human-like creatures were hanging there from iron meat hooks. He often shut himself up inside. It was cool in that shed, and no one disturbed him there. The creatures were losing their blood drop by drop. And the soft sound of it dripping on the floor helped him endure his situation with fatalism.

The organic things were terrifying; they had bloated bellies that were black and dried out, full of shrivelled roots. The face was horrible; it was a demon's face. A face of wickedness, with two large, listening eyes. Much had been written about death, but this kind of death remained unwritten.

He had gone hunting in the mountains. The ones who changed always went to the mountains. They were drawn to these mountains from blind instinct, from noseless, eyeless instinctual drives for nourishment, self-preservation, and reproduction. The mountains craved them. Craved the animal, vegetable, mineral, physiochemical side of these horrible, slimy, hairy things. And at times, when he had begged over a dozen or more, he felt pity, or rather, he at the very least felt no hatred for them. He believed, or he wanted to believe, or he couldn't *not* believe that, in some ways, he disliked his dark work, and then again, in other ways this terrible work was intoxicating.

Blood was dripping. There was blood on the stone floor. A yellow phosphorescence in the blood glowed gently in the setting sun.

The entity was giving off a peculiar odour, nauseating, sweet. He could smell the blood, much redder than the blood of other animals. It hung in the air, this sweetish smell of earth, of leaves sprouting and trees rotting. He asked himself how he could stand the sight and smell of that blood. He didn't know what had happened to him to be able to do this and, in a sense, he had no idea what he had done. Perhaps he had done something evil here. He had always suspected that he was evil. That the world was itself evil, intrinsically evil, evil by its very essence. He hated life. It was not worth living. And this wasn't because he was sick—as everyone had always said, all his sad childhood, when he had been suspected of perhaps not being fully human—but because he was cowardly. A coward. There was a sense of relief in knowing that he was just a coward and that life was evil.

He could see the blood on his white hands. He knew they were dirty but the sight of his hands covered in blood made him feel better. Otherwise, he would have been lost completely. The entity's eyes had wept blood. Blood had come out. It had to come out. Oozing at the eyes, ears, nose, and mouth. It was coming out everywhere, everywhere as blood.

He was reluctant to eat the entities. The worshippers who ate them had grown sick. The region was poisoned by the strange roots stirring in the crops, which the entities alone could digest. So the entities, decomposing slowly in the cold shed, were soon unhooked, quickly to be thrown into the river that flowed out of the delicate green forest, where they drifted downstream to an even greener sea, and continued to flow, as everything flows, a long time.

Afterwards, he washed his hands in the river. They were very dirty. The water was cold. He didn't feel much like washing them. Because he didn't need to wash them. Because washing them wouldn't solve anything. Everything inside him came up against his crime and struggled against its gigantic dimensions. No human could bear its weight. But he could not have cared less about the survival of a doomed species. Only the manifestation of the will, its nature and the planet it inhabits, its eternal becoming, its eternal flow, would last this accursed instant. Nothing would last longer. Forever and again, the will only endured. The world that betrayed him would also survive him.

In the sound of the river he could already hear eternity rushing toward him in the distance. This gift, this body, this earth, was a curse.

●

Like a figure out of apocalyptic folk art, Johannes Van Vyferyken stood in the field with a broad hat darkening his face, observing the plowed acres as dark as black bread. In the valley, between the mountains and the sea, the land was being cultivated. Prisoners were regularly transported from other Canadian labour camps and installed in a village built on a place called Johannes' Marsh near the vast acres of lowland and forest.

He read the lists that the government sent him from the farm office without a second thought. The lists of victims were varied—kind, reserved, intelligent, timid people. He had been using their system of lists to keep track of these prisoners at the collective-farm. A new list from another camp would arrive every three weeks or so, sometimes a month. And they just kept coming. In that order: first the lists and then the prisoners. Rapid transport trucks streamed in from all over the continent. Groups of skeletal prisoners arrived, and then, everything repeated itself in the same way that it had with the worshipers before them.

The whole crop flourished. A dopethrone. Property of SynBio's pharmaceutical division. When harvest time arrived, working together, the prisoners gathered what had sprung up out of the earth's darkness. The crop, originally the brownish-pink colour of rosewood, had later turned a yellow mottled with green, and it wasn't long before the skin tone of those who worked out on the plains became that same green. Rotting the harvest on the stalk, as it wasn't the crop's yield that they were reaping but the symbiote. Offering the root wrought greenery all there was to give.

It always began after that.

In the middle of the blackened mud, human skeletons were scattered by a bulldozer's blade. There was no escaping those frightful fields, those who had worked them were stranded, stranded amid chequered stretches of evil life: fear, madness, fever, and oblivion. Instead of wheat, crops of corpses. Corpses thick on the ground, hundreds of corpses, rotting in the sun. Their mouths pale against the Canadian earth. The earth stunk. It was disgusting. It had the stench of bloated cadavers, swollen, organic entities.

Shuddering in the face of his work, this stifled and gasping deterioration of the set of functions that resisted death, Johannes Van Vyferyken felt a sense of dissipation at all he had achieved. He did not know exactly where the feeling came from. It was a strange, troubling feeling. As though dark saturnine forces had pushed him, some inverted incarnation that had spawned within the calcified depths of his heart through the black roots of the stars themselves.

The prisoners never noticed. They never noticed what had been concealed in their bodies, what had dwelt there. Asleep and awake. At first it was the texture of their skin that degenerated and then came the loss of speech, the effect on the shape of their body followed, their anatomy, their respiratory and circulatory systems becoming no more than a jumble of organs in slow decomposition. All they felt was time sinking and sinking, until they returned to the plain as the wild forest, as the fruits of the mangrove trees. When they died, they were buried in the ground, in the plains. All around them was the pure wildness of terra incognita. The prisoners themselves were terra incognita. The land was terra incognita. Terra incognita was everywhere.

The truth, the glow, the fall. Again and again: Dead. Dead. Dead.

At midnight, the headlights of long-distance trucks met near the collapsing face of a red barn. The pseudo-human heads were shaved, they were put into civilian clothing, all the while, looking at nothing—not the truck they were being loaded into, not each other, not anything. They had reached emptiness's peak. What remained of them was a stiff, inert manikin and the hope only of empty vessels. All were the strange pink and green hues that had been in the land. And yet, they were alive. Or at least not unalive.

Their death was not useless. They would be used. No longer requiring anything besides functional sensory equipment, they would be deployed. The function of these silent, motionless, powerless, paralyzed observers would alone be to perceive. Johannes Van Vyferyken was their necromancer, whose dead magic resurrected a future regime of fascist zombies, a civilization that was coming to an end, in the same way all great empires before it had; not through the suicide of its people, but the omnicide of their spirit. Come election day, a class of corpses would fill the streets. The election would take place. And a threatening future would emerge from the darkening past. There would be no more difference between the living or dead: they were one and the same.

The American cities were schizophrenic, crowded as they were, with people wearing sickness masks because online conspiracy theories told them that the chemtrails of airplanes were seeding clouds with psychochemical agents and god knows what else.

"Bacterial blooms," they said, with a crazy look in their eyes, "extracted from the Venusian atmosphere during the NASA mission and then injected into our own." These people—who suffered from more than just seeing bacteria colonies gather in mysterious dark spots that changed shape, size, and position over time but never disappeared—not only distrusted the government but distrusted other people and distrusted themselves most of all. And who could blame them, after all that was happening to them? They were witnessing their doom.

"I witnessed doom," Jaegwon Choy said. He heaved a deep, deep sigh and threw his head back, thinking of the dark and difficult days that lay ahead.

He found himself on the evening pavement that skirted the refugee quarters of Germany, where thousands of squinting pupils were peering intently at the earth. Germany, more than any other European country, felt on the edge of a civil war. *It won't be long before war breaks out between the Slavic countries and greater Europe, chiefly because of the refugee crisis, caused or worsened by the embargo*, he thought, and then the thought boiled over from inside him as a feeling. A feeling unknown to him until now: the feeling of a frantic mind. But unlike all the other ignorant frogs that hadn't noticed the gradual rise in temperature, he was ready to jump out before his system of passive anticipation became lethal.

When the whistle was blown, no one had heard. Not right away, anyway. It had made sense to give himself up to the so-called enemy for safekeeping. But they hadn't wanted to listen; half of his solicitations hadn't gone anywhere; the other half had struggled from office to office.

•

He and his documents were butted from one line to another. Until he finally met with one of the strange men in uniform leafing through thick files. He asked Jaegwon Choy several meaningless questions and that was it. Several months went by in this way. And in a series of official and unofficial requests, Jaegwon Choy asked, demanded, that his return to Korea—where his daughters were, he emphasized—be helped along.

He was certain that soon he would be making his way to Korea, but not before he answered the German intelligence agency's questions concerning his involvement with Biosphere II. They would come to an arrangement.

But what was he supposed to tell them? If he had stayed in America, he would have been taken to the labour camps or perhaps deported to a USENA space colony on Mars—the planet for ethnic resettlement—and end up worse than these people here in the immigrant quarters: subtracted and without even a toilet.

Every day Jaegwon Choy walked halfway across the city, past the barbed-wire entanglements that surrounded the refugee camps. The EU compounds, those gloomy fortresses in the slums, were wreathed with the corpses that had tried to break through the steel rings. Those who worked as monitors among them were ready to put any of them to a violent death.

Isolated and surrounded by the barbed wire, by madness, by the unknown, the refugees called to him for help with illiterate hands, using gestures that spiralled slowly upwards, it being necessary for them to describe "Help!" with and without words, somehow knowing he wouldn't understand their language alone. Their hands showed an abstract form, perhaps symbolizing the cause of their suffering, and how it appeared to the eye. A spiral, a shape peculiar to springs and certain staircases, the motion of their hands like a snake coiling around nothing. But he didn't understand this description either. There was nothing concrete about it, nothing clear about it. Just this talking spiral, a circle that rose upwards but never closed, a vertical circle that repeated itself as it rose but never reached fulfillment, caught up in this senseless orbit around nothing. He thought and did nothing. Because they were indistinguishable in the vast vortex, the vortex in which the whole world indolently wallowed.

Their eyes seemed to mirror all the world's suffering. They needed help and he had no help to give them.

Jaegwon Choy walked on, encountering occasional patrols. Some let him pass; others studied his documents with the glowing end of a hand-rolled cigarette. They looked like dead people, and they smoked like dead people, too. That dead world was a world of doorknobs. He shuffled on, hugging the walls. The air was choked with soot and smoke from hundreds of industrial pipes sticking out of stone and glass factories, buildings that seemed to be breathing through a multitude of tracheas.

There were long lines for everything in Germany now. Jaegwon Choy was on the streets, where the chaos was multiple. The lampposts were badly spaced and broken groups of people hurried past. The rest of Europe's open societies, nearly bankrupted by their attempts to cure the onset of yellow peril or perhaps, for Germany, late orientalism. Theirs was the kind of psychocultural fear that had brought both pseudoscience and Nazism to plague European society in the early twentieth century. Passive, timid, morally uncompromising, and dominated by feelings of guilt, the political consequences of being economically dependent on China went mostly undiscussed. Europe, in an attempt to link itself to Africa and forge a new industry for their migrant workforce, proletarianizing them into the new working class, had begun the one-hundred-year process of building a dam and then draining the Mediterranean. All out of the medieval fear that the Mongol invasion of the West was repeating itself through Easternization. Europe was in critical debt, and Germany was their only creditor.

Like Germany, the Americans were obsessed with the whole picture, the gestalt. Perhaps more so than the Germans. The Americans, with their advanced global surveillance systems and cosmic exceptionalism, had certainly taken it to yet another extreme.

The American government, a government that had returned to the brutalism of the early twentieth century, had let them know nothing. That is, nothing the public knew about that catastrophe was true. And yet, by a simple process of elimination and rationalization, Jaegwon Choy knew everything. Because he had been there at the point of origin: a constellation of points, all connected, all important.

•

Before he absconded from America for amnesty in Germany, Jaegwon Choy had found the lateral roots and adventurous shoots of organic rhizomes forming their intricate microbial nets through the unbelievably black topsoil of the university greenhouse. Soil containing bacteria with the same plasmids that were found in the biosphere. Lotus flowers in half-blossom were the size of eyes, and their swelling buds grew, grew relentlessly out from where the students' true eyes should have been. Under their human skin was a wondrous jungle with veins like lush tropical growths hung along overripe organs, and weed-like entrails writhed in squirming tangles of red and yellow from rock-grey lungs to golden intestines. Underneath it all, flailing between liver and light, was the bird of their new soul.

They have turned, Jaegwon Choy had thought, stunned by what he had seen, *into the image of thought.*

•

Later, in the transcription of Jaegwon Choy's interview, recorded by the German intelligence agency, the interrogation officers read, reread, and then read again the Korean-American philosopher's confession. They read it as though it were the screenplay for a science-fiction film submitted to a studio in Hollywood, and they, the directors, had to try to understand how it would all come together on the screen.

In a strangely lit interrogation room, with hauntingly luminous shades of pale blues, pinks, and yellows refracting off the walls and the ceiling's rounded vaults, Jaegwon Choy felt his sense of distance evaporate as it would have under a light installation's electric photons or in a blizzard. Here he told the German interrogation officers his story of decision and indecision and nondecision.

"Schiz-o-analysis?" the German interrogation officer on the right said, testing the word in English. The word seemed unnatural in his mouth.

"Schizoanalysts, unlike psychoanalysts and their Freudian arborescence, believe that meaning can be represented by four circular components that bud and form rhizomes," Jaegwon Choy said, with a twinge of defiance in his flat voice because he was being recorded. "That is, there is no conceivable sociological, hierarchical, psychosexual, or even neurological power structure in what schizoanalysts are studying."

The officer on the right nodded, knowing when to let something go. They had the file and could research the term later.

"So in relation to the project, you were hired to study the effects of the experimental serum on the biospherians during the course of a two-year experiment, and you were not physically present for many of the recorded trials. You were told it was the first experiment of its kind, though, officially..." He opened the file and consulted the existing transcripts; the edge of the paper-clipped-pages that gave his most vital information showed clear.

Jaegwon Choy shrugged. "Officially. There could have been other iterations. I don't know. I was in the dark about that."

"Why would an AI system choose to trust you with private information stored in someone else's AI wrist console?" the German interrogation officer on the left asked in French, touching the object intentionally placed on the table between them. The other officer bit his lip, scratched his nose with his pen, and again rummaged through his papers.

Jaegwon Choy's expression told the officer what he thought of the question. "I don't know," he said, a note of irony in his voice now. "Just as the fate of the mountain gorilla depends on human goodwill, maybe the fate of humanity depends on the actions of machine intelligence making decisions and goals that align with some humans and conflict with others."

The interrogation officers exchanged a few solicitous words in German. No one was looking at the same person at that moment, and it felt a bit like everyone had a gun pointed at someone else beneath the table.

The officers leaned forward. "How much was done before the door was opened?"

Jaegwon Choy nervously answered the second nonrhetorical question, which surged up toward him like an attack from the officers as their recording devices hummed. "A lot"—he decided to try again—"but not enough to have prevented all of this from happening."

He told them that the biosphere's space farm was among the highest producing in the world. The biospherians had extended their life spans through diet alone and, using the technosphere system, had managed to maintain a healthy environment of biogenerative technologies and life systems. He knew these things based on the statistics he had extracted from the AI wrist console.

"You know, I look at the Santa Catalina Mountains almost every day." Video footage was playing in the background. Jaegwon Choy remembered the telegenic man who had said this into the camera, remembered his peculiar almond-shaped eyes and the distinctive hardness of his jawline beard; he didn't have to be shown the footage. He had already watched it to death. "You can see them through the glass walls of this place's ceiling when the crop dusters aren't spraying the fields with that lemonade-yellow fog. I feel afraid when I see them. Most people might regard those mountains as freedom, perhaps a glimpse of the natural world. Not me—I know better. I can see they are cleared of their trees for housing and property, and I can imagine the dusty eucalyptus leaves on the boulevards and the smoke billowing from the mouths of ugly power plants and the interstate's noise that must echo in the foothills. Those people wouldn't know how to live in those mountains if they were still mountains. This, in here, is all we have left of the natural world. And if we don't succeed in our mission, then neither do those people on those mountains." The biospherian forced a sour smile and then raised his glass and shook the ice cubes therein, which clattered like hollow bones. "We are all of us on borrowed time, in one borrowed place or another."

The biosphere's AI surveillance system had constantly monitored the biospherians' psychology in the confined environment. Unfortunately, scientific politics and infighting, outside and inside the biosphere, had resulted in factions of the eight-member crew of biospherians. Some had known too much; others, knowing too little, had assumed the others were wrong. Despite this, the biospherians had maintained a metabolic connection to the biome, an interconnectedness, and interdependence with their own personal Gaia.

"So it's OK to make a promise," the biospherian woman had said to a surveillance camera, screwing up her face in a mixture of amusement, confusion, and disgust before twisting it into a reckful grimace. "But it's not a good idea to keep one?" After the factions were created, there was almost no interaction among them in the common area without some kind of yelling, hollering, or heckling, as if they were on death row. They had begun communicating with those outside the biome, bribing whoever they'd had on the outside to smuggle in something: a cell phone for one, tobacco for another.

Despite the faction, the eight biospherians had a visceral bond to their life-world and demonstrated this in a profound way: by keeping air, water, atmosphere, and health in their attention constantly.

"If every child in America had a vivarium growing up, they wouldn't need their parents to explain what we're doing here. Actually, I built my own. That's right, a vivarium in a vivarium in a vivarium—can you imagine that?" The biospherian had said this to Augustus Lovejoy's angled fisheye lens, which scowled at him from an electrical outlet, its glowing red light making a record of his work. He had presented his model vivarium as though it were the winning experiment for biophysics at a state science fair.

All the biospherians had fit the explorer or adventurer profiles, similar to astronauts, and although they had thought they experienced depression, they had shown no actual signs of it. But like all isolated groups, they had exaggerated psychological problems and unconsciously, perhaps inevitably, sabotaged each other and the overall mission.

The biosphere's AI system had been designed to choose whatever actions appeared to best achieve its set of goals. Not knowing what the utility function was, Jaegwon Choy assigned himself to watch what the AI watched. Watching what the camera watched. Observing the biospherians as they displayed what schizoanalysts referred to as the generative, the transformative, the diagrammatic, and the machinic components of the rhizomes becoming, in jargon terms, rhizome-beings.

"I needed the names for things that aren't, and these flimsy terms got me as close as I could get," Jaegwon Choy said, with a look of indifference and no answer from the German interrogation officers. They simply scrutinized him more closely, in silence, and then buried their noses deeper into his papers.

The eight biospherians had begun as concrete human beings. And then, as the experiment progressed, they had started to mix with their environment and had become the pure tracings of other beings. They had accreted more and more of the environmental information, until, like geckos, they had camouflaged right out of sight. Becoming the colour of air.

One of the German interrogation officials took out a sheet of paper and ran his finger down the lines of writing. He stabbed at it at one point and showed it to his colleague, who then fixed his eyes on Jaegwon Choy and boomed at him, pausing the television at what would have been the opening to a second act: "What do you think is happening to them?"

Jaegwon Choy gave the unexpected answer, the television's dark medium showing them what lies beyond the possibility of human sense, and by functioning too well at showing them that world, the footage somehow breached that unbridgeable gap between the objects being mediated.

First, because the biospherians had spent much of their time in the anthropogenic biomes (the habitat of human living space designed for them to separate themselves from the six other biological biome areas), their physiological features had shifted, phenotype by phenotype, and skin pigment and facial attributes had altered their colour and shape and form.

When the sexes of the subjects changed, so did their behaviour. A biospherian who began as a male or female would either switch or transcend the binary completely. Some had even become emotionally and psychologically transsexual. Eventually they all were hermaphrodites, and later still, their genitals became ambiguous, which offered increasingly novel forms of sexualization within the anthropogenic biome. In some cases, the genitals disappeared entirely, going dormant or inactive or asexual. Those of the latter classification had the most tendency to embrace change, experiencing more aberrant hallucinations, which took the study into its furthermost reaches, for the hallucinations guided the rhizome-beings' entanglement.

Among those who had experienced these changes in anatomy, some decided that if they went into one of the six biological biomes they would risk losing control of their human selves entirely. And so, the group of eight biospherians factioned off from one another, under the pretense that those who left could never return, for what they might have returned as was still in question.

Coming into contact with the serum would completely resequence a species' genetic sequence into the biological hardware of another species. The genetic sequences were hacked and recorded to express potentials that were never originally there and emerged, making the new content physical.

In short, the biospherians who had left the anthropological biome developed phenotypic anomalies that made them into a part of the very biome they occupied: an orchid in the rainforest, a coral reef in the ocean, mangroves in the wetlands, a few green spikes of grass in the exhausted dirt of the savannah, or a wasp in the desert fog.

Along the lines of these first bizarrely uncanny but otherwise peaceful tracings came the budding of the abstract machines themselves, and in turn, the marvelous assemblages that effectuated these abstract machines became fully conspicuous. Jaegwon Choy called these assemblages of organic machines "the horror"—a name that he pronounced in the Latin, *horrere*—slurring it slightly, as if reacting to or expressing an emotion rather than imparting information. Creatures no longer human, with monster faces up their arms, that evolved and devolved at incredible rates, progressing from one level of consciousness only to regress into another, into the pure terror of space.

Given the absence of any further questions, Jaegwon Choy exchanged glances with the German interrogation officers and posed one himself. "Have you ever shuddered?" He asked this through his feelings of blind anxiety. The officers did not say yes or no and so he went on, reflexively quoting Theodor Adorno: "That shudder in which subjectivity stirs without yet being subjectivity is the act of being touched by the other."

This potential for the organism to retrogress at the loss of all form—a wilting after the budding—proved to be a prevailing threat over those who managed the project. And of course, the breach in Biosphere II, by an ex-biospherian of the second expedition, successfully made that threat a terror.

●

After having turned it over in his mind, Jaegwon Choy sent them a coding sequence that linked into the video surveillance camera of the biomes. The security footage of the break-in of Biosphere II was inconclusive. The perpetrator wore a gas mask, which made it hard to prove who it was, definitively. But for him it was obvious. No one, besides someone who'd had previous access to the facility, could have done what this man had done in the time that he had done it.

Johannes Van Vyferyken, like an insect-faced monster, moved from one of Augustus Lovejoy's cameras to another in full biohazard gear.

Cam Op. 1: A window is broken, alarms and sirens wail, and the armed guards who travel the perimeter in their truck don't know where to focus their attention. A biological agent is loose. The land beneath the other blown-out windows of the habitat is covered with growths that no one wants to get near. The glass walls, still intact, have dripping washes of graffiti—"Where is Nature?" in bubbly white letters.

Cam Op 2: On the other side of the facility, the biohazard-suited figure is entering in the pass-key combination. The airlocked emergency door opens. He walks inside, leaving the door ajar.

Cam Op 3: Bypassing the other biological biomes, he reaches the anthropogenic biome.

Cam Op 4: Once in the lab of the anthropogenic biome, he scans the room, then begins a thorough search through the cold storage. After finding the serum, he takes one sample and puts it in a cooler he's pulled from his backpack. The cooler, which looks like a miniature silver rocket, is the size of a thermos. He destroys the rest of the batch on the spot.

Cam Op 5: He takes longer on his way out. To Jaegwon Choy, he seems warier of crossing paths with whatever is still inside with him. The biohazard suit stops abruptly, after something sounding like the shrieking, screaming, yelling, or moaning of a woman begins. The camera catches a strange colour precipitating, and a patch of ground close to the man moves, camouflaged in the breeze patterns of the rich yellow grasslands of the savannah biome. The screaming woman resolves into an animal: a mountain lion. He remains motionless and then reaches out his hand, his palm turned upward; he appears to be whispering something to the listening mountain lion as it sniffs his hand. The mountain lion gives the impression that it understands his words and looks at the camera looking at it. The mountain lion changes its shape, transmogrified, and then two grey foxlike forms appear, passing into opposite directions, their lustrous tails trailing after them. The biohazard suit leaves the same way he came, shutting the heavy door behind him. By this time, fifteen minutes have passed. The guards have missed him.

The German interrogation officers turned off the television, picked up Jaegwon Choy's file, nodded at him, and walked out the door.

•

Jaegwon Choy shared what information he could with the German intelligence agency, who in turn promised him safe passage to Korea. An agency that, after Jaegwon Choy's interrogation, immediately planned their pivotal role in taking preventive, logistical measures against what they thought could ultimately amount to a kind of cosmic pessimism, which needed to be quarantined.

The Event, that philosophical concept that Jaegwon Choy had dedicated his life's work to perfecting, had been reduced, classified, and therefore understood and communicated by the German intelligence agency to the German government and the Eastern Alliance as an intrusion. Or, as Jaegwon Choy wasn't ashamed to admit, an alien invasion.

The true horror for Jaegwon Choy was that his theory might be right and his thoughts constituted some kind of action. The fact that they lived in an age where thoughts increasingly turned to actions terrified him all the more so. "Thought police seem necessary after all," he said in a defeatist way, and would have willingly pleaded guilty to his thoughtcrime had Orwell's Oceania been a real place. Maybe it would be some day.

Because thought is not human.

All at once, he was gripped by the certainty that he understood completely—better than he had ever understood himself — and that he was finally able to go home. He would make his way home, more aware that this time his intellectual life really was over. But home was no longer there, for, in order to protect his family, he was required to surrender his identity. And so, after a series of lengthy surgical procedures, he had been effectively post-racialized.

As soon as that information entered the system, Jaegwon Choy knew that he had brought the Event to the rest of the world. Not through any kind of pathology in his body—that was only the physical manifestation and would remain contained to North America—but through a pathology of his mind, which was much worse and would outlive him considerably.

The philosopher Karl Popper had a way of explaining this: there were three worlds. World one was the world of physical objects; world two of mental objects; and world three of the objective spirit: knowledge, values, culture, and its artifacts—the symbolic order within which we all share value and meaning. This third world meant that an image, once introduced, must exist to the end. Activation was possible, deactivation was not.

World three was what most people missed, not being able to look past the concreteness of the first two. This third world would, in time, create a whole new world—the solution to the event determining the event—based on the idea that destroying America was the right thing to do. Without considering just what it was the Eastern Alliance was destroying. There were no "signs" Jaegwon Choy could use to help the German intelligence agency understand and communicate this ultimate reality, like an artist could through a painting. Only an immense range of accumulated time could do what he had failed to do.

In time they will know because they will occupy the Event and the Event will occupy them, Jaegwon Choy thought, as he left the German intelligence agency to determine their own fate. He watched as the owl of Minerva spread its wings with the falling of the dusk. *No, history has not ended. Nothing has ended for us.*

And when the good genius born in them counts the good deeds with white stones, and the evil genius born in them counts the bad deeds with black stones, they will attempt to tell lies to one another, and say that they did not commit any evil deeds. But then, and only then, will the Lord of Death consult the mirror of retribution and then, and only then, will the karmically created hallucinations they were deluded by come to an end.

Terrorism was anything that affected political choice: explosions, hostages, invasions, mass shootings, cybernetic attacks, and bioplagues. All had terror as their political affect. *So, a rapid extraction of the facility's contents, specifically the serum from Biosphere II,* Johannes Van Vyferyken thought, *was an act of domestic terrorism.* But what Johannes Van Vyferyken had taken and what he had produced for Augustus Lovejoy's own monopoly of violence were two sides of the same double bind. A two-sided image between which he had to choose: the one, was an intimate terrorism, the other, a power-sharing deal amongst rivals; though the two were notionally equal, this was rarely the case in reality.

Johannes Van Vyferyken served a forgotten danger. He served Augustus Lovejoy. His ignorance of this had become sacred, and this ignorance went by the name of forgetting. However, he could not forget his time during the takeover, between his management position with Space Biosphere Ventures and his temporary contract with the Institute of Ecotechnics.

It all came back to him.

Johannes Van Vyferyken felt that his movements there, on the side of memory that retained his unconscious choices, were now returning to him. And because he was now within that incomprehensible place in the interior part of himself, in his character, in his nature, some great inner change had already taken place. It was in this place that he had become heavy, with too much gravity.

It all came back to him: how he had pressed the buzzer and tapped out a code on a pad next to a door; how he had shown his card to a camera so that the door would open; how he had stepped in and then through another door. He had walked into an elevator; behind his back the first door closed with a loud bang. The elevator descended with a small quiver, and once in the basement, it opened its doors. Across from him was another door, and finally a third door. He took one step into a huge room, a room where he found Augustus Lovejoy with company. *Company* was not the right word; Augustus Lovejoy stood in front of a humanoid creature that had been manoeuvred into an armchair.

"Close the door. Sit down and watch closely," Augustus Lovejoy said.

Johannes Van Vyferyken was rooted to the spot. His lost eyes dashed from the homunculus, to Augustus Lovejoy, to the tiny dispenser on the table.

"But... I don't understand," Johannes Van Vyferyken mumbled.

"You will shortly. It had the immunization two weeks ago. I just injected the thing with a gram of the serum concentrate. Now stop talking nonsense and pay attention. It is, after all, your immunization treatment. Look. It's beginning to stir."

The homunculus twitched in an odd way, thrust out its chest, and clenched its fists. Its eyes remained closed. Then foam began to bubble from its lips; it opened its eyes and held them open. It stared dully at Augustus Lovejoy and Johannes Van Vyferyken. Then, with an animal cry, the homunculus leaped out of its seat and hurled itself at Augustus Lovejoy. They rolled across the floor, knocking into table legs and overturning chairs. Johannes Van Vyferyken rushed up to the ball of tangled bodies and, brandishing a clenched hand, struck the homunculus with a violent blow on the temple.

Augustus Lovejoy struggled to his feet, gasping for breath through bloodied lips. "Tie it up. Quick."

As Johannes Van Vyferyken was knotting the rope around the hands of the homunculus, it began to stir like a person awakening from a long and deep sleep.

"Tie its legs," Augustus Lovejoy snapped, spitting blood on the floor. "I don't need another scuffle."

Bound hand and foot, the homunculus opened its eyes again. Its body convulsed, but the convulsions did not resemble the spasms of a raving lunatic. It did not scream; it merely whimpered and sobbed, quietly and plaintively. Its empty blue eyes streamed with tears. Augustus Lovejoy, regaining his composure by degrees, drew his chair closer and regarded the homunculus with a slightly mournful smile: an unsentimental tenderness, a bland, empty compassion.

This homunculus, the first, was one of many incarcerated felons—felons who had been transferred from various federal penitentiaries and used as lab subjects. Their former illnesses came gushing out of their brains and flooded their muscles; every homunculus, like the first, ended up thrashing furiously on the secret laboratory floor. Terribly incomplete. The immunization had not worked and would continue to not work because the plasmid had already mutated beyond their understanding.

After an intense attack of vomiting, Johannes Van Vyferyken's forehead was relieved, fresh and cold. Vomiting those last human remnants. He was no longer afraid of someone entering the room, but he had the much broader dread of someone who has already entered. He had abandoned his post.

Being truthful about the way people die is the embodiment of nonviolence, Johannes Van Vyferyken thought. *When it came to the storage of plutonium after decommissioning hundreds of nuclear units globally, it was suggested that plutonium could either be stored deep underground with militarized warnings or in knives and forks without any warnings whatsoever.* The same could be said of measures taken by those in control of the serum: the organism was reduced to a bland substance that could be manipulated at will without regard for unintended consequences.

Johannes Van Vyferyken's plasmid appeared the same at the molecular level as every other plasmid, but with distance and time, sameness became difference. *Logically: viruses came before bacteria. Thoughts before minds. Hallucinations before thoughts. Flowers before plants. The earth precedes the tree as the world precedes humans. The matter of the body precedes the body, just as reality precedes the voice that seeks it. Patterns before evolution.* This was the mesh. Invisible nonhumans and nonplants installed at profound levels of humans and plants. Circular disks. Plasmid molecules. And if the molecule could make a pattern, the possibility for there being conditions under which self-replication was able to spread through heterosexual cloning became a fact with considerable purchase: that is, the introduction of plasmid DNA into an isolated mitochondrion could be used for bioterrorism.

Johannes Van Vyferyken felt ambivalent: the guilt, the shame, the melancholy, the horror, the ridiculous, the ethereal, the hollow, the sadness, the longing, the joy. He couldn't tell whether these layers of himself were something old or something new; they seemed to be both, as if the past's history and the future's history were destined to meet at some random and unpredictable point. That point of bliss for him was somewhere between metabolism and metamorphosis.

Ergot-contaminated grain resembles a tiny black banana a few millimetres long. It grows naturally on the seed heads of grain and grass plants. Ergot bodies are formed in place of grain kernels, so ergot development is detectable during kernel formation. However, infection occurs long before the ergot bodies are visible. Once there is visual confirmation of ergot, you can't do anything to stop the infection in the crop.

The ergot alkaloid was introduced into the genetically contaminated seed. The fungus overwintered in the hard bodies, and in the spring, it germinated and formed mushroom-like structures that produced spores. Honeydew containing millions of these spores was then dispersed to other florets by insects like butterflies flying along their usual migration routes.

The ergot bodies rarely survived more than one year in the soil. And a year was all the Machiavellian prince of fear, Augustus Lovejoy, needed to create the embargo.

●

If Céline Høltermand could find him, so could anybody else who really wanted to. So could, he was willing to admit, Augustus Lovejoy.

He remained trapped. Trapped in that narrow circle that nature had drawn so completely, with such irrevocable finality, around him. This shell kept its shape despite the series of subtle variations that pain and time inevitably wrought over one and the same human life. He was what he was for himself in the theatre of nature. That was all he would ever know. He would essentially remain unchangeable.

In the face of the repeated failures of his work, he, at times, felt the sacrifice of his life had actually been in vain. It was in failure, and through failure, that the omega point had been reached. Limited by the human sciences, he had exploded the casing of that claustrophobic circle. By preserving the error he had found hidden within the language and concepts of the scientific sector, he had forcefully introduced his incomplete system of genetic derivations, and then put that error into the earth, like grain lying hidden inside it, patient and potent, with the wild hope, the paradoxical desire, that what had been sleeping would swell and come to life, to go beyond the filth of humanity. But nobody escaped the narrow limits of their being and their consciousness, and neither would he. His fate couldn't improve. Fate was cruel, humans wicked.

The morning after Céline Høltermand left, Johannes Van Vyferyken walked the property line with a finger through the ear of his mug's handle. Big globs of rain fell from the sky and formed dark spots where they landed. Soft explosions. The tea from his mug was like a meal inside him. But it wasn't just the tea; it was as if everything was a meal inside of him, deepening things, making them transparent with their light inside.

At the bottom of his cup, the tea leaves showed what messy metaphysical wisdom they had to offer. It looked like the dense swaths of a forest burning greenly, and that was all he could read from it. His reaction to the serum was doing this to him. The total spell that transcended the spell, and by transcending it also transgressed. The spell of this life coming to a penultimate truth: that the end was also a beginning.

In his other hand, he dumped out another jerry can of gasoline, and the earth swallowed it, instantly.

Heightened sensory impressions were already reducing his ability to calculate and generalize. He was fading fast. Seconds mattered more than minutes, and hours were impossible. He had to do it now. So, he sparked a large match on the bottom of his boot, lighting first his pipe and then everything else. Like electricity through wire, the fire caught and moved. The gasoline combusted into an actual flame and sparked in one thousand places. It was burning. All of it. All of it burning and transforming. And as it transformed, so too did he.

All true exits require a regression. Anything is possible since we know nothing. But we don't come from nothing. Because somewhere there is something.

Inside Johannes Van Vyferyken there was also a burning that rolled through every cell as it spread throughout his entire body, pieces of him rolling away forever in all directions. A cellular experience of bonding between beings. Hollow shafts formed the shape of feathers followed by their hairy afterfeathers, which sprang loosely from each goose bump. His head was now covered in ravendark feathers and his bones went hollow. Fingertips grew long and what had been his palms scooped the air like shovels and fanned the nest of flames. He was lighter than air. Weightless and floating. His thin hands winged and hovering. From his face, a beak protruded only as much as it integrated, merging his nose with his upper lip and his chin with his lower mouth so that his words became as hollow as his bones.

The avian hours of his blue peace. Only his eyes retained human intelligence. Human eyes that looked down from his avian form as it spiralled in the updraft, in a corkscrew motion that gyrated toward the sky and away from the Earth. Away from the godforsaken Earth and its godforsaken people. Away from the wicked love that burned like a fire inside and outside of him. Away. Forever, away. Into the ashen mesh.

His hazy humanoid blot began its slow descent into the flames, so that the only thing he was aware of now was the hot, bitter taste of reality on his palate and in his aching limbs. He disappeared in a single flash, reduced to nothing but a jumble of mean dots arranged in directionless spirals.

They found her vehicle. The gaping mouth of the glove compartment was open. Its various contents—tampons, tissues, Tylenol—littered the passenger side. They found the broken camera at the birch grove before they finally reached the shore.

Approaching the edge of the forest, the operatives glimpsed a strange shape at the water's edge; it turned its human skin inside out, exchanging smooth flesh for striped fur and barrel chest, to become a great mass of orange and black. A monstrous creature, and yet somehow like the shape of a woman. A shape that made them tremble.

The shape moved fast, in a powerful, muscular motion, suddenly shifting from the shape of a woman to that of a beast, intellect to sinew and claw. A dark orange blur, rippling against the trees like a procession of shadows.

The semblance of a tiger materialized and burned brightly before them as they stood apprehensively, some in camouflage and others in black suits, like a murder of crows. Among them, Augustus Lovejoy alone maintained his composure with a kind of dark tranquility as he swallowed mouthfuls of heavy shade from the shadows of trees that lay in his path, piercing him like spears.

The sunlight changed as it shone through the predator's piercing amber eyes. The tiger smelled the blood in their veins and purred deeply.

Augustus Lovejoy unholstered the gun resting tight against his hip, aimed, and pulled the trigger. Like a lightning bolt coming out of his fingertips, the bullet left the gun and plunged deep into the tigress's bulk. Bloodstained, lead-free ammunition ricocheted around the fissure and raised great sparks from the rock as it struck through to the shore. The red shock that came with the sight of blood made him feel adrenalized.

The tigress, though moving with the wasted motions of a partially destroyed insect, easily closed the distance between her and Augustus Lovejoy. She distended her jaw to reveal a wet red maw full of sharp teeth, which plunged into Augustus Lovejoy's head, tearing it off at his shoulders. The tigress chomped and chewed through throaty growls and torn flesh. Bit into him like a pomegranate, at once bursting open the rind and spilling the red jewellery of its seed. The blood purpled the ground; the pulpy chambers held the bright citrus flavour of orange, the pith bitter.

The transformation did not end there. The immortal hand of the drug that had turned the woman into a tiger then turned the tiger into hundreds of rabbits and the rabbits, like the white-crested waves of the surf, flowed into the ocean and drifted into the sky and never died but continued to be, until there was nothing left for Augustus Lovejoy's operatives to grasp of her, for only the traces of that former being remained: a radius of blood. A mystery hidden within a form that passed through their hands like a shadow into the nameless place beyond.